Sheesh, he

Alec grinned slig[...]
see you have som[...]
Celia."

Celia scowled. "How do you do that? Read my mind."

He shrugged. "We've got some kind of chemistry going, whether you want to admit it or not."

She lowered her eyes. "Actually, that's part of my...um, problem."

"Your *sexual* problem?"

Heat rushed into her cheeks, but she knew he was deliberately rattling her, so she lifted her chin and forced herself to meet his gaze. "Yes."

His attention shifted to her breasts, and her nipples immediately peaked. His eyes narrowed. "Everything appears to be working just fine."

"That's part of the problem," Celia admitted. She swallowed hard, searching for the right words. "You...you look at me, and I forget all my convictions."

He stared at her incredulously. "You mean your sexual problem is that you *want* me? What's wrong with that?"

"Sex without some kind of emotional commitment is just sex!"

"Which can be damn satisfying!" he replied, pulling her into his arms.

Dear Reader,

When I first introduced Alec Sharpe in my September book, *Beguiled*, (Harlequin's 50th Anniversary Collection) he was just supposed to be a secondary character. A quick on-and-off-the-scenes kind of guy. But somehow, even when off scene, Alec's presence hung with me. I like him. A *lot*. His mystique, his short, blunt replies, his dark masculine aura, all added to his appeal. In my mind, if not on paper, he became a full-fledged hero, worthy of his own book.

Celia, another character from *Beguiled*, just sort of forced her way in as the heroine. She butted heads with Alec right off—with no direction from me! Their relationship took shape before my eyes. When I decided to write *Wanton*, the story was already there, fully realized, begging to be told. All I had to do was type it.

It's not often books come to a writer so easily. Usually, when they do, it means the characters are special. I think these characters are very special. I hope you do, too! I'd love to hear from you—you can write me at P.O. Box 854, Ross OH 45061. Or e-mail me at lorifoster@poboxes.com.

All my best to you!

Lori Foster

P.S. Look for my next Temptation romance in March 2000!

WANTON
Lori Foster

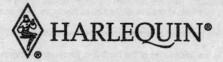

HARLEQUIN®

TORONTO • NEW YORK • LONDON
AMSTERDAM • PARIS • SYDNEY • HAMBURG
STOCKHOLM • ATHENS • TOKYO • MILAN • MADRID
PRAGUE • WARSAW • BUDAPEST • AUCKLAND

If you purchased this book without a cover you should be aware
that this book is stolen property. It was reported as "unsold and
destroyed" to the publisher, and neither the author nor the
publisher has received any payment for this "stripped book."

To my sister, Monica Flowers. Your constant support
means more than I can ever tell you. Not only do you
show up at book signings, you actually buy my books!
(And you seem happy to do it!) Thank you, Mo.

ISBN 0-373-25852-6

WANTON

Copyright © 1999 by Lori Foster.

All rights reserved. Except for use in any review, the reproduction or
utilization of this work in whole or in part in any form by any electronic,
mechanical or other means, now known or hereafter invented, including
xerography, photocopying and recording, or in any information storage
or retrieval system, is forbidden without the written permission of the
publisher, Harlequin Enterprises Limited, 225 Duncan Mill Road,
Don Mills, Ontario, Canada M3B 3K9.

All characters in this book have no existence outside the imagination of
the author and have no relation whatsoever to anyone bearing the same
name or names. They are not even distantly inspired by any individual
known or unknown to the author, and all incidents are pure invention.

This edition published by arrangement with Harlequin Books S.A.

® and TM are trademarks of the publisher. Trademarks indicated with
® are registered in the United States Patent and Trademark Office, the
Canadian Trade Marks Office and in other countries.

Visit us at www.romance.net

Printed in U.S.A.

1

CELIA BIT HER LIP. She felt naked in the tight, flesh-toned dress, too made-up with the cosmetics that had spent more time in her drawer lately than on her face. She was very aware of her bare thighs, of her exposed arms and cleavage. Though the air-conditioning hummed, she felt warm with embarrassment.

Heads turned appropriately as she sauntered through the dim interior and took a direct path to the bar. She didn't want to look too closely, but she was sure Mr. Jacobs, the slime, was here. She had his description and knew this was his prime picking ground. This was where he chose the women. Hopefully, he'd choose her as well.

Slowly sliding onto a bar stool, she worked to gain his attention. Her heart pattered rapidly. Though she couldn't deny the underlying fear she felt, she also relished the excitement, the anticipation...the end satisfaction. It had been laughably easy to leave her old *proper* life behind, though her relatives were still having a hard time accepting it. They expected her to show up at the company office any day, dressed in a business suit, hair neatly tucked away in a functional, professional style, begging for her old job back. Ha.

It didn't matter that no one thought she could do this. All she had to do was prove to herself that she

was capable, that she wasn't too pristine or squea-
mish to see the job through. That she could make a
difference in some other woman's life. She'd do that
tonight.

It was a nice enough bar, she thought, smiling at
the bartender as he took her order. They made idle
small talk, and she slipped in the fact that she was a
woman alone, new to town, without relatives or
friends in the area. He lingered, subtly, politely, asking her more questions. How long would she be in
town, did she have a job. He cautioned her to be careful, and she almost laughed. He worked with Jacobs,
she was sure of it.

Sipping at the drink she didn't really want, she
watched him walk away. Cool air from a ceiling fan
brushed her bare thigh where her dress had parted at
the side slit. Ever since they'd locked her fiancé away
for crimes too horrific to think about, she'd done all
she could to forget her carnal appetites, to deny an
overly sensual nature. Yet here she was, prepared to
do her damnedest to get a man's attention by using
her body.

Surreptitiously, she glanced down the length of the
bar to the small round table located there, situated in
the far shadows. The man occupying the table, blond
and very good-looking, perfectly matched the description she had been given. It was easy to recognize
Jacobs; he had the same classic, refined, golden-boy
appearance as her ex-fiancé, a look she now recognized as slick and phoney.

It took all her control to keep from reacting as he
surveyed her through narrow, contemplative eyes.

His gaze skimmed over her from her loose tousled hair down to her high-heeled sandals. Not wanting to be too obvious, to look too anxious, she turned her head away and flipped her hair over her mostly bare shoulder.

Seconds later her pulse jumped, then raced wildly as she sensed the approach of a man. She didn't turn to look but she could feel the tingling awareness of him, could detect his male scent, not in the least subtle. Yes! He was going to take the bait. Her palms began to sweat in nervousness but she ignored it. She felt him brush against her while taking his own stool, and that brief touch felt electric, making her jump in surprise. She struggled to moderate her accelerated breathing. He was looking at her; she felt the burning heat of his gaze as strongly as a firm stroke of flesh on flesh.

Mentally rehearsing the speech she'd prepared, she turned to face him, her smile planted as she leaned slightly forward to display as much cleavage as possible, given her small size. Her gaze slowly lifted, met his, and she froze in horror. "Oh no."

"Hello, Celia." The low, barely audible words were said in a familiar growl through clenched, white teeth.

"Oh no."

His smile wasn't a nice thing and sent gooseflesh racing up and down her spine. His eyes locked onto hers, refusing to let her look away, and his lips barely moved when he spoke. "Close your mouth, honey, or you're going to blow your own cover. And I don't feel like fighting my way out of here tonight. But then again, seeing you in that dress, a fight might be just what I need."

She snapped her mouth shut, but it wasn't easy. The eyes looking at her weren't blue, weren't admiring, and didn't belong to the man she was investigating, the man still sitting a good distance away, now watching curiously. These eyes were too familiar, a cold, hard black, and at that moment they reflected undiluted masculine fury.

Her heart raced even faster, urged on by new emotions, new sensations. She felt nearly faint, and collected her thoughts with an effort.

Forcing a shaky smile that actually hurt, Celia whispered, "Just what are you doing here, Alec?" She tried to make it look as if they were merely conversing, getting to know each other. She needed to maintain her camouflage, damn him, and Alec knew it.

Rather than offer an answer, he tossed back a handful of peanuts from the bar and watched her. His black hair—taken to curling toward the ends—hung loose tonight to touch his wide shoulders and reflected the glimmer of colored bar lights. Those same lights shone brightly in his narrowed eyes, eyes that made many a man back up in nervousness without a single word being spoken. His sharply cut, ruthless features seemed etched in stone, accurately reflecting his mood. He even smelled of danger, a hot, spicy, masculine scent that appealed to the senses, even as it amplified her nervousness.

Everyone in the bar seemed to be looking at them, waiting, but then Alec often got that reaction. He exuded menace, and people picked up on the silent threat quickly. He was a man who wore his tiny gold hoop earring and tattoo without artifice; the small decorations merely seemed a part of the overall man. His requisite jeans, scuffed boots and black T-shirt weren't exactly appropriate dress for the upscale bar, but Celia doubted anyone would be brave enough to ask him to leave.

She was brave enough. "Look, Alec—"

His dark, devilish gaze did a slow burn down the length of her body, effectively stifling her protest. He paused on her small breasts as they rose above the neckline of the dress, thanks to the wonders of the push-up bra. She shifted uneasily.

He smiled, not a reassuring sight, and his attention snagged again on her tummy. She felt that look inside herself, then more so as his intense scrutiny lingered on her exposed thigh.

She wanted to smack him for rattling her so, but then she always wanted to smack Alec. He confounded her and angered her more than any man she'd ever met. But worst of all, he made her feel the undeniable reactions of a woman just by his mere presence, and she resented it. She didn't want to want him, not when something inside her was a little afraid of him. He wasn't an easy man, wasn't domestic in the sense of the average male in today's society. When he looked at her, when his black eyes met her own, she sensed a certain degree of savage wildness, of primal masculinity that couldn't be tamed. She always hesitated to push him too far, and that angered her more than anything.

"Answer me, Alec."

His smile was again more taunting than comforting. "I suppose I'm here to save your stubborn little behind, though to tell you the truth, that's not my first inclination. At least, not where your posterior is concerned."

She sucked in a startled breath as heat flooded through her. What in the world did he mean by that? She couldn't quite tell if it was a threat of physical punishment, which she could easily ignore, or a sensual promise, which would be impossible to ignore. Alec did that all the time, made those suspicious little comments that stirred feelings she didn't want to acknowledge. Her one liaison of a romantic nature had ended in tragedy, and made her determined to ignore her baser instincts. They had overruled her common sense once, but never again would she put the people she loved in danger. Now she wanted to help protect women from bastards like her ex-fiancé. But her experiences with him, while making her wiser, hadn't in any way prepared her for a man like Alec Sharpe.

When they'd first met, he'd made his interest in an affair, and his disinterest in marriage, well known. Celia wasn't inclined to indulge either one, so she'd done her best to disregard his attentions—not at all an easy feat considering Alec was an impossible man to disregard on any level. But then she'd left her family's company and joined her brother's private investigations firm where Alec worked. He'd had a fit, appointing himself as her bodyguard, dogging her every step. Nothing had been the same since. Especially not after she'd gotten him shot a couple of weeks ago.

Celia winced, her guilt still keen. "Uh, should you be out and about on your leg already?"

His eyes narrowed, the obsidian depths almost hidden by long, sooty lashes that she envied every time she looked at him. "That's right, this is the first time I've gotten to see you face to face since that bullet hit my leg. Were you worried about me, sweetheart?"

That purring undertone had her defenses rising. Alec ruthlessly used every available opportunity to wear her down, to point out her shortcomings. She shook her head and feigned a casual interest in the bar. "Not at all. Your hide is as tough as nails and Dane said it was only a flesh wound."

"Yet you've still been avoiding me."

"Don't be ridiculous. I've just been...busy."

Alec reached out and caught her chin, bringing her face around so she had no choice but to witness the seriousness of his gaze. Her heart tripped, her senses coming alive with the simple touch. "That bullet was meant for you," he said, his tone low and rough, rubbing along her raw nerve endings. "If I hadn't been there, you would have been shot. I thought you might have learned your lesson then, but obviously you're not as bright as I first figured, considering you're here now."

That was an insult she couldn't let pass. She started to jerk away, then remembered her audience. She desperately wanted this case, wanted to prove she could handle herself while helping others, and if she got into an argument with Alec now, her cover would be blown. Dane had taught her that was the most important thing, the strongest safety measure. She had to remember to stay in character or she put not only herself at risk, but also the client and the other agents—in this case, Alec.

So she leaned toward him instead, seeing his nostrils flare and hearing his indrawn breath as her lips came within a millimeter of his own. Her heart thumped heavily with her daring, but she was getting sick and tired of him playing caretaker, constantly checking up on her. She still thought it was mostly his own fault for getting shot. He'd distracted her by his unexpected presence, otherwise she would have seen the threat before it became a reality.

She felt his incredible heat, smelled his musky, male scent, and felt his breath brush her parted lips. She stared into his dark eyes point-blank and a sense of sheer feminine daring filled her, almost obliterating her nervousness. It was like facing down a wild beast, exhilarating but also terrifying, making mush of her insides.

Against his mouth, she whispered, "I'm smart enough to know you have no say over what I do or don't do, Alec Sharpe. So why don't you just pretend you're not interested in me tonight, and head on back wherever you came from so I can get on with my business?"

Rather than backing off in anger as she expected, his long hard fingers slid from her chin to the back of her head where they tangled with her hair and wrapped around her skull, locking her firmly in place. She saw his small, satisfied smile before his lashes lowered, hiding his eyes. In response, Celia's own eyes opened wide in alarm as she belatedly realized his intent. Too late.

His mouth, hot and deliciously firm, closed over hers.

Slow, softly biting, inexorably consuming, the kiss obliterated all thought. The world seemed to come to a shuddering standstill as his mouth devoured hers, hot and easy. She didn't hear the quiet droning of the bar, no longer felt the bar stool beneath her or the cool air-conditioning on her skin. She lost awareness of the man she was here to investigate. Nothing penetrated her fogged mind but Alec and what he did to her, how he made her feel.

Good grief, the man could kiss.

His teeth teasingly nipped her bottom lip, and when she gasped for breath, his tongue licked inside, then plunged. She moaned in sheer surprise and excitement. He tilted his head, fitting their mouths more surely together and she thought she might have helped him with that, reaching blindly for him. The kiss seemed to go on and on before he finally pulled back, releasing her by slow degrees with soft, tiny kisses meant to appease. She was so stunned, he had to pry her clutching hands from his shoulders and put them in her lap. Her first reaction was regret that he'd stopped—but it was quickly followed by the hot lash of shame.

It had been a long time since she'd been kissed, forever since she'd been kissed like *that*, and she'd responded as if starved. She squeezed her eyes shut and tried to deny the truth about herself, but she couldn't. She had hoped the awful ordeal with her fi-

ancé had cured her of her overly passionate nature.
But Alec, a man who didn't care for her, who relished
insulting her and tried to bully her at every turn, had
gotten an even stronger response from her. How
could she have kissed him back like that, losing all
sense of time and place and purpose? Where in the
world was her pride?

It took her precious minutes to get her bearings
again, to hide the embarrassment that threatened to
bring her low. And when she did, Alec was helping
her off the stool. He had her purse in one fist, had
paid her bill, and was leading her out. He walked behind her, automatically protecting her back, she
knew, constantly nudging her forward.

Oh no. She hadn't accomplished a thing yet! She
stiffened, but Alec's hand came around her waist and
curved over her belly. The thin material of her dress
was no barrier against the hot hardness of his large
palm. His long fingers spread, spanning her from
hipbone to hipbone. She sucked in a startled breath in
response and retreated backward, attempting to pull
away. But that only brought her up flush against the
front of Alec and she felt his tall, hard body all along
the length of her back. His erection, so blatantly obvious, pushed against her bottom. She felt a new,
wilder rush of heat and she locked her knees against
the tightening curl of desire.

Alec bent and his lips brushed her ear. To the onlookers, it appeared to be foreplay. To Celia, it was a
sizzling threat. "Don't look back or you'll give yourself away. Every man here, including the ones who
count, figure I just made arrangements with you for

the night. That was your objective, and for the moment, keeps you safe." He pressed his mouth to her temple in a strangely tender kiss, then added, "From them."

From them. Meaning she still had to deal with him and that was much more alarming than what she'd faced in the bar. But she knew he was right. For now, there was no salvaging the night. She could come back tomorrow and hopefully her ruse would be validated by Alec's actions. Mr. Jacobs, the blond, blue-eyed villain she'd been trying to meet, would see her as a desperate woman alone, an easy pick-up.

Celia forcefully snuffed out the small voice in her mind that claimed the ruse a reality. The kiss with Alec was a mistake; she wouldn't let it happen again. She wasn't desperate, or easy—not anymore. She was only determined to see the job done. One way or another, she'd keep her overheated sexuality under control, and she'd nail the man who was ruthlessly ruining young women's lives.

Mr. Jacobs picked up women who seemed to be alone, telling them he wanted them to model for him. Some of their photos might even make it into a small-circulation magazine or two. But that wasn't what he really wanted. And Celia intended to prove it. She only hoped she'd made an attractive enough picture to draw his notice. Combined with the conversation she'd shared with the bartender, she hoped to have left enough bait.

Forcing Jacobs to show his true colors, exposing him to the authorities, would be an absolute pleasure. But her first priority, for now, was saving one young woman in particular. She couldn't forget that; she couldn't forget Hannah.

As Alec led her to his truck, she thought about what she would say to him. The night air was warm and humid in mid-July and the sensual haze lifted while she felt her skin grown damp beneath the slinky dress. He was still behind her, still pressing her forward, and she wanted to run. Alec Sharpe, her brother's number one agent, had kissed her senseless. He had curved his big hand over her belly and she could still feel the imprint of it there though he'd moved it away when opening the door. She felt like an animal.

"I can get home on my own."

Without explaining how he knew it, Alec said, "You didn't drive, and I'm damn sure not letting you get on a bus or wait for a taxi."

She twisted to face him. "You have no say in what I do."

His eyes flashed down at her, then skimmed her body once again. "Wanna bet?"

They waged a silent battle for all of three seconds, but Celia knew she didn't dare cause a scene so close to the bar. Anyone might see, and then questions would be asked, questions she couldn't afford if she wanted to handle this case without complications, without embarrassing Hannah further.

Taking her silence for acquiescence, Alec opened the truck door, lifted her by the waist and plopped her inside. He dropped her purse on her lap then slammed the truck door, and without a single care, strode to the driver's side and slid in.

Damn it, she'd known since the day she met him he was trouble. It didn't matter that her brother, Dane, trusted him more than any other man he knew. It didn't matter that her sister-in-law, Angel, actually let him baby-sit her sweet, innocent little son. It didn't matter that he always got the job done, that he had never hurt her, that he had in fact taken a bullet meant for her on the last assignment she'd botched.

What mattered was that he was lethal to her senses. He had kissed her, and she'd liked it. But his kiss had been meant to remove her from the bar without fuss. He'd used that kiss against her, just as her fiancé had used her sexuality against her. And it had worked.

She couldn't, wouldn't, let herself get involved with him. For the past year-and-a-half, she'd effectively put her sensual, prurient nature under wraps, and she wanted to keep it that way. As soon as she got home, she'd call Dane and make him intervene. She hadn't wanted to do that because it felt too much like tattling, like using her relationship with the boss to get special favors. But this was crucial.

She had sworn off relationships after her last disastrous attempt at finding romance. Lust had blinded her to reality then, and the shame was still a part of her. But she was now older and wiser and determined to forge a new life for herself while making amends for past mistakes. *Without sexual involvement.*

Dane was going to have to make Alec leave her alone. That was all there was to it.

2

"PUT ON YOUR SEAT BELT."

Alec was aware of her unease, but he wasn't ready to comfort her yet. He hadn't been kidding when he'd issued his less-than-subtle threat to her posterior. When he'd found her in that bar, playing at being a damn tramp and looking ripe for the part, he'd wanted more than anything to turn her over his knee. But he figured if he ever did have Celia Carter in such an interesting position, punishment would likely be the last thought on his mind. He knew he could never hurt her; hell, he'd taken a bullet rather than let her be hurt. But all other possibilities were still wide open. The things he did want to do to her were numerous, and driving him nuts.

Especially since she seemed to make a career of telling him no—about everything. As a result, he was learning to live with constant frustration.

He could almost feel her gathering her courage. She did that a lot with him and it amused him. Grown men had been steering a wide path around him since his late teens, but not Celia. Right from the start, she'd tried her best to stand up to him, but always there was a touch of fear in her mellow hazel eyes. She'd rail against him, give him hell, but with obvious nervousness. To him, the fact that she stood up to him despite her fear indicated a hell of a lot of guts and he admired that in a woman. In fact, he'd admired a hell of a lot about Celia Carter since first setting eyes on her.

What he didn't admire was her impetuous race for adventure that had kept her on the edge of danger ever since she'd left her family's secure company and joined up with Dane. He still couldn't figure that one out. So her fiancé had turned out to be a grade A bastard? There were plenty of them in the world to go around, and it certainly wasn't Celia's fault that she'd been too innocent to see through Raymond's scam. Alec had already been working with Dane to nail Raymond for numerous crimes, not the least of which was the murder of Dane and Celia's brother. At the time, they hadn't known for certain that Raymond was the culprit, but they'd had their suspicions. In the end, Celia was the one who'd saved the day, sneaking up on Raymond and clobbering him with a tire jack while he'd held Dane and Angel at gunpoint. Celia had more than vindicated herself in everyone's eyes.

Everyone's but her own.

Alec knew Raymond had hurt her tender feelings, trying to use Celia as a pawn in his schemes. It was the worst emotional insult a man could deal a woman, using her that way. She obviously felt horrible for having ever believed in him. In truth, Alec wondered what the hell she'd seen in Raymond. He'd disliked the man on instinct the moment he'd met him. But then he was good at what he did, and he'd been doing it a long time. The same wasn't true of Ce-

lia. For the most part, and despite her loud claims to
the contrary, she was still a wide-eyed innocent.

So why the hell did she want to risk her damn neck
day in and day out trying to prove something? The
anger washed over him again, fresh and raw, and he
growled, "You're not going back there, so you can
stop your scheming right now."

Her head snapped around toward him and she
glared. "I'm going to talk to Dane. You're not my boss
and I want you to quit acting like you are."

Primal satisfaction settled deep into his bones.
With this one woman, he wanted every advantage he
could get. "Now there's where you're wrong."

He felt a return of her wariness. He was so painfully attuned to her and her feelings, he always
seemed to know what she was thinking and feeling. It
unnerved him, even as it turned him on and made
him more determined to have her. There was a link
between them that she did her damnedest to deny.
He wouldn't let her do that much longer. When she
was lying naked beneath him, he'd see to it that her
thoughts were centered solely on accepting him and
the incredible pleasure he'd give them both. There'd
be no room for doubt or denial.

"What are you talking about?"

He tightened his hands on the wheel, pressed his
foot to the accelerator and relished this moment of
proper balance between them. He hadn't liked it
worth a damn that Dane was her ultimate boss, leaving him no say-so in what Celia did or which job she
chose. That had finally changed, and not a moment
too soon, given where he'd found her.

Luckily, the darkness hid his smile, but the satisfaction came through in his tone. "With Angel pregnant again, Dane's decided she needs an extended vacation. He's rented a house in the Carribean and he's taking the family there for a month. While he's gone, I'm in charge." He slanted her a look, saw her shock and decided to clarify just to make sure there were no misunderstandings. "So you see, Miss Carter, I am your boss."

"No."

He took great pleasure in nodding. "Afraid so."

"I won't have it!"

"You, Celia, have no choice." Her hands fisted, her entire small body going taut in automatic rebellion. He wanted to pull her close, to cuddle her and reassure her; they were soft urges he hadn't experienced with a woman in fifteen years and he didn't welcome them now. He firmed his resolve, blocking out all the weakening, tender emotions. Protecting Celia was for her own good, so he'd do it whether she liked it or not.

"Listen close, honey. If I find you even thinking about that particular case again, I'll fire you in a heartbeat. As a matter of fact, from here on out, I'll personally give you which assignments I want you to have. And you can bet they won't include dressing like a hussy and putting your sweet little ass on the line."

He finished that grand statement with a flourish, pleased with himself and his implacable stance. But when he slowed the truck for a turn in the road, Celia unsnapped her seat belt and opened the door.

Cursing, Alec slammed on the brakes and tried to steady the wheel. The truck shuddered to an immediate, bone-jarring halt. Alec saw red and reached for her, the idea of getting her over his lap more appealing by the moment. But she was already leaping out, her own anger giving her the advantage of speed. She landed awkwardly on her high heels, fell to her butt, then jerked quickly to her feet again. If his reflexes hadn't been so good, and he hadn't stopped the truck so quickly, she might have broken her neck. Waiting for the truck to actually stop hadn't seemed like a concern to her.

A middle-aged couple who'd been walking by on the dark night stopped to stare. Alec saw Celia dust herself off, nod at the people, then start briskly on her way, limping slightly.

He quickly maneuvered the truck to the curb, jerked out his keys and trotted after her. *Damned irritant.* Her brother was sharp as a tack, reasonable, calculating. There wasn't an impulsive or careless bone in his body. Dane always knew what he was doing, and how he was going to go about doing it. He and Alec worked perfectly together, both of them practical, methodical, *sensible.* So where the hell had Celia gotten her foolhardy, damn-the-consequences attitude?

Alec grabbed her arm and held on while she tried to jerk away. She swung her purse at him and he dodged it. "Just settle down, damn it, before you hurt yourself."

"You bullying behemoth, get your hands off me!"

The names she called him usually made him grin.

But not this time, not when he had an important point to make and already knew how resistant she was going to be. He clasped both her arms, effectively immobilizing her. Through clenched teeth, he growled, "Just this once, Celia, will you please use your head?"

"I am using it," she insisted, her eyes and cheeks hot with temper. "I'm going to go to the corner and hail a cab, and from here on out, I want nothing to do with you. You think you're going to fire me? Ha! I quit."

The pedestrians, still enthralled by the drama taking place in front of them, moved on quickly enough when Alec's darkest, most threatening glare shot their way. He pushed Celia into a small storefront doorway, out of the path and view of anyone else out wandering the streets on this blacker-than-pitch night. The corner streetlamp didn't quite reach them, and they were isolated by the darkness.

He forced himself to take three deep, calming breaths. Her statement that she wanted nothing to do with him had cut like a knife and left him bleeding. Damn her, she would not shut him out. Not anymore.

"You're being unreasonable," he finally said, doing his best to keep his tone calm, to hide his own anger. No one, man or woman, had ever set him off like this, but then it had always been that way with Celia. She elicited more emotion from him, in all forms, than anyone he'd ever known. She could make him furious with a word, amuse him with a burst of temper, or arouse him to the point of pain with a simple shy look. He didn't like it, but more than that, he wasn't quite sure how to deal with it, and feeling

helpless was something he hated above all things.
The only way he could see to get over it was to finally
have her, to sate himself on the scent and feel and
taste of her. He could easily spend a week doing just
that, and he eventually would. But first he had to insure her safety.

"Do you want to get hurt?" He shook her slightly,
both hands now holding her bare shoulders. He was
careful not to bruise her, but he wanted her attention,
needed her to know he was dead serious. "Do you realize what could have happened to you last time if I
hadn't gotten in the way of that bullet?"

She lowered her gaze and stared at his shirtfront.
He had the almost overpowering urge to press his
lips against the part in her fair hair. She was so damn
baby soft all over. Soft hair, soft skin...*soft smell*. His
chest suddenly felt tight, his muscles rigid, and he
fought against it, against the effect she had on him.
The need to kiss her, to eat her alive, was strong. He
wanted to make her a part of him so she'd quit fighting so hard.

He gave her another quick, careful shake. "Celia?"
he demanded in a growl.

"That was an accident," she muttered, her voice
quavering slightly. "I thought the guy was just jumping bail and that he'd be easy enough to bring in."
She peeked up at him, her hazel eyes wide and vulnerable, swallowing him whole and making his
hands shake. "I didn't mean for you to get hurt."

His fingers flexed on her shoulders, stroking, relishing the tender feel of her warm flesh. A slow burn
started in his gut. "Celia...damn it, that's exactly

what I'm talking about. You don't know enough yet
to get involved in cases like that. They'd grabbed that
guy on petty theft, and he was small-time, but he
knew bigger, more dangerous guys and you bumbled
right into their dealings by following him without
backup. You didn't wait for a partner the way you're
supposed to and you didn't call the cops when you
should have."

She swallowed. "Does...does your leg still hurt?"

It wasn't his leg bothering him. He thought about
lying, pondering whether his injury would have any
effect on swaying her to stay away from danger. But
he doubted it. She was so damn headstrong and unreasonable. "No. It's fine."

"Nothing keeps you down for long, does it?" She
peeked up at him again. "You're so invincible."

Hardly. His hands tightened again, because
around her he felt like a naked baby in the woods, but
damned if he'd admit it.

"I just wanted to prove I could do it," she whispered, reacting to his anger.

Her words made him want to explode. *"Why?"*

She drew a shuddering breath, and his attention
was diverted to her breasts. He wasn't sure how it
was done, since understanding the working of
women's underwear wasn't high on his list of accom-
plishments, but her small breasts were fairly bursting
out of that damn dress. They taunted him, when usually it was her pert behind that grabbed his undivided attention. That and her unwavering stubborn-
ness, which he admired even as he resented it.

"You wouldn't understand, Alec."

Probably not, since he'd forgotten what the hell they were talking about. He wanted to pull the plunging neckline of the dress two inches lower so he could see her nipples. Would they be pale pink, or a dark dusky rose? He could almost taste her in his mouth, her sweet flesh puckering tight. His erection strained against his jeans. Lord, if just thinking about kissing her breasts made him shake with lust, he wasn't sure he'd actually be able to survive being inside her. He closed his eyes in self-defense and swallowed hard. But shutting out the reality of having her in his grasp only allowed him to dwell on the fantasy of getting her beneath him, warm and soft and ready.

He groaned.

"Alec?"

He forced his eyes open, saw her worried gaze, and frowned. With one fingertip, he tipped up her chin. "What wouldn't I understand, babe? Explain it to me."

She licked her lips, leaving them wet and shiny. "I need to make a difference. I've screwed up a lot in my life, hurt a lot of people."

Her self-recrimination did a lot to dispel his lust and clear his brain, so that her words held all his attention. He started to correct her, to tell her how wrong she was, but decided to let her talk it out instead. Later, he could set her straight.

"I almost lost Dane, and I did lose Derek because I was too dumb to see Raymond for what he was. My entire family was hurt, the company was hurt. Innocent people were victimized. The only way I can live with myself now is if I help someone else."

Alec smoothed his fingers over her cheek, tucking a blond strand behind her small ear. Her hair was soft and fine, with natural curl. "Hooking up with Raymond was a mistake, but we all make them. You can't expect yourself to be exempt. And you can't undo the past."

"I can try to make amends."

"To who? Dane knew what he was getting into, and you couldn't have helped Derek even if you'd known. You didn't even meet Raymond until after Derek had died."

It was an awful situation, one Alec knew she still hadn't come to terms with. She'd only been a stepping stone in Raymond's plot against her family, but of the survivors, she'd been emotionally hurt the worst. Raymond had started with industrial espionage, and quickly advanced into more deadly crimes. It had taken all Alec's fortitude to allow the law to have him, rather than utilizing his own sense of justice. He could have taken care of Raymond without an ounce of remorse.

Celia turned her face away. "I feel like I betrayed them all."

His heart twisted, and the pain was so unfamiliar, he jerked. Slowly, his hands flexed on her smooth shoulders, pulling her closer, which made the pain less noticeable. "Celia," he whispered, the word a reprimand breathed into her ear, "you know that's nonsense. Dane loves you, so of course he doesn't blame you. And Angel adores you. You've become her best friend, a godmother to little Grayson."

Her small hands lifted to his chest and lightly

rested there. Her forehead touched his sternum. "I can't believe she's forgiven me. It's because of me that Raymond was able to threaten her." She tilted back to stare up into his face, and her belly pressed against him. "She could have been hurt—"

"Hush." He laid a finger over her lips, fighting the urge to taste her again. That first kiss, meant as a showdown, had made him hard, and being near her had kept him that way. She'd tasted sweet, like cherries, but now her lip gloss was gone and he found her naked mouth even more appealing. "You're not responsible for Raymond's actions, Celia. And the truth is, you saved Angel by showing up when you did and wielding that tire iron like a pro."

He smiled and she managed a skimpy smile in return. "Regardless of what you say, Alec, I know I hold part of the responsibility. And it...it disgusts me so much, knowing I was engaged to that animal, that I might have married him, that I *did* sleep with him."

Alec froze, not wanting that image to invade his mind, but it was never far from there anyway. The thought of Celia having sex with Raymond sickened him and filled him with a killing rage. He dropped his hands and took a step back, trying to distance himself both physically and mentally. He didn't want to care who she'd slept with, as long as she slept with him, too. But it wasn't that simple and he knew it.

He loomed over her, ready to intimidate once again. "You won't change anything by getting yourself killed. Do you think Dane deserves that right now, after he's finally found happiness with Angel and the baby?"

She wrapped her arms around herself, holding tight. "I've learned my lesson. I'll be extra careful from now on. But when I saw this case, I knew I had to do something."

"Damn it, Celia!" His frustration exploded, but he recognized her stubborn look and knew there'd be little chance of changing her mind.

She glared at him, her chin jutting out at an obstinate angle. "Well you just refused it without even giving Mrs. Barrington a reason why!"

In her pique, Celia no longer looked so vulnerable or so small. She stood barely five-foot-six in her heels, a good ten inches shorter than him. But when she gave her anger free rein, she reminded him of an Amazon.

She clutched at the front of his shirt. "Do you know she thinks her daughter is involved in *prostitution*? That she's been forcibly coerced into it? Hannah thought she was joining a modelling agency, but now—"

"Spare me, Celia," he said in disgust, his anger rising once again. "I read the case and I interviewed Mrs. Barrington myself. Her daughter was a spoiled brat who left a very loving family behind to chase the limelight. I've heard it before. Hannah wants to be famous, and she'll likely do whatever it takes to see it come true. Mrs. Barrington just can't believe her precious daughter would willingly stoop so low. But it happens. There's no one to save this time, and Hannah likely wouldn't appreciate your intrusion into her cozy little life-style, anyway."

Celia thumped her fist, still tangled in his shirt,

against his chest. She looked outraged and appalled. "You're not even willing to check it out?"

"I just told you, I already have." He covered her hand with his own, holding it tight against him. "Trust me on this. I know more about it than you ever will and I have eons more experience."

"What does that mean?"

Damn it. He swiped his hand through his hair, unwilling to tell her just how much experience he had with a situation such as this. Even thinking that far into the past made his head hurt. He narrowed his eyes and made his tone deliberately cold. "You've wasted your time coming here. Now let's go. We'll stop at the room you rented so you can pick up your stuff, and then head home. No reason to spend another night here."

He had her halfway to his truck before she dug in her dainty heels. "I'm not going with you, Alec."

His patience was at an end. He turned to her, then bent down until his nose was almost touching hers. "Yes you are. If I have to haul your stubborn hide over my shoulder and tie you in the damn truck, so be it. But one way or another I'm taking you home. Now."

Her small body practically vibrated with anger, her eyes hot with it, and then her eyebrows lowered ferociously. "All right. I'll come with you. But I'm not giving up this case."

"Then you're still fired."

"I still quit," she qualified, and slid into her seat. She didn't look at him, but stared stonily ahead.

Alec braced one hand on the dash and the other on

the roof of the truck. He leaned in close, using every intimidation tactic he knew. "When I inform Mrs. Barrington you're no longer with the agency, do you think she'll still be willing to pay your expenses?"

Celia curled her lip, for the moment too angry to be cowed by his excellent routine. One long manicured finger poked him in the chest with stinging force. "Fine. You do that and I'll just work gratis. But one way or another I'm going to find out what's going on with Hannah Barrington. I'm going to find out if her mother's suspicions are correct. *I'm going to help that girl.* And you, Alec Sharpe, can't do a single thing to stop me."

Alec got out of the truck and slammed the door, afraid he'd strangle the little witch if he stayed that close to her a second longer. She knew how to push all his buttons. No one, male or female, had ever seemed to take so much delight in provoking him. Hell, most people were afraid to try! It wasn't what he was used to, what he was accustomed to dealing with. Damn it, he wanted to see this at an end. He wanted Celia Carter kept safe.

He wanted her—period.

What a horrible situation to find himself in. He couldn't do it, no matter how hard he tried, but he knew it would be best if he just stayed the hell away from her. From the day he'd met her, he'd seen all the signs. Miss Celia Carter was trouble with a capital *T*, and he had the bullet wound to prove it.

3

THE RIDE TO HER MOTEL was made in absolute silence before Celia decided she couldn't take it anymore. Alec was being so boring, she was about to fall asleep. The quiet, along with the dark night and the breeze from the open windows were proving to be very hypnotic. She wasn't even all that mad anymore. Alec couldn't help being the way he was. His bossy arrogance seemed an innate part of his nature. And overall, she accepted that it was concern which prompted his temper. *Concern for her.* He was one of those incredible men who thought everyone smaller or weaker warranted his protection, and nearly everyone was smaller and weaker than Alec. Not that she would allow him to boss her, but at least she could understand why he wanted to try.

What had really kept her quiet for so long was the way he'd pulled away from her when she'd mentioned sleeping with Raymond. Evidently the awful truth of what she'd done, of what she'd allowed Raymond to do, disturbed him as well. But she couldn't fault him for that, either. No one could disparage her horrid judgement any more than she did.

The quiet had given her plenty of time to think, though, and she'd come to several conclusions. She didn't like it, but she was forced to face the truth. She needed Alec's help.

Staring at his hard profile, she sighed. "So are you going to brood all night?"

"Yes."

She almost laughed at that, her mood lifting slightly. He was such a big, dark, awesome man to admit to actual brooding. But she could see he was more relaxed now, too. That ever-present aura of danger that loomed around him like a thick black cloud had softened. His hands were no longer gripping the steering wheel as if he might snap it in two, and his jaw wasn't as tightly clenched.

Celia smiled at him, hoping to cajole him into a more agreeable frame of mind. "I have a sort of 'off the topic' question for you."

He gave her a suspicious look, his black gaze cutting over her features before he reluctantly shrugged. "Go ahead."

"How did you know where I was? I made a point not to drive, to take the dumb slow bus instead so people would see my car in the driveway and think I was still at home." She didn't mention that the "people" she'd most wanted to elude was Alec. But as usual, he was one step ahead of her.

As she spoke, he pulled into the motel parking lot where she'd rented a room. Celia shook her head in amazement. "And how did you know I was staying here?"

He made an impatient sound and shut off the truck's motor. "I'm a P.I. This is what I do."

He shifted in his seat to face her, one long arm

stretching out along the back of the seat, almost touching her. The darkness of the cab's interior closed around them, relieved only by the lights of sporadic traffic. She could smell his scent, feel the warmth of his big body. His arm with the tattoo was closest to her, and she glanced at it. It was too dark for her to see it clearly, but she'd studied it many times and always wondered at the significance. A man like Alec didn't tattoo his arm with a heart, pierced by an arrow, for no reason. She just didn't have the nerve to ask him what that reason might be.

She shifted restlessly in her seat. "But *how?*" she demanded, going back to her original question. He narrowed his gaze, his look calculating, and she warned, "Don't you dare lie to me, Alec."

One finger touched her hair, twining around a loose curl, unnerving her further and filling her stomach with sensual butterflies. He watched his hand, his dark eyes glinting in the soft moonlight. She saw the moment he decided to tell her the truth. His shoulders lifted in a slight, unconcerned shrug. "I broke into your house and found your travel plans."

Her mouth dropped open and she stared at him in utter disbelief. She took refuge from his overwhelming nearness in the flash of anger that jarred her wits back. "*You did what?*"

Disgruntled, he released her and opened his door. Celia scrambled out her own side before he could circle the truck, then stepped in front of him, hands on hips, chin thrust out, blocking his way. "You broke into my house?" she demanded, injecting as much outrage in the words as she could. He ignored her and she had to quickly backstep since he didn't stop, then was forced to skip to keep up with him.

"I didn't do any damage." He said it as if that would be her only concern, as if the invasion of her privacy was nothing at all. He glanced down at her, then added, "You need an alarm system. I'll take care of it when we get back."

Celia slung her purse strap over her shoulder and clasped both hands around the back waistband of his tight jeans as he started up the outside stairs leading to her second-floor room. She dug in her heels, but only got dragged in his wake. "Damn it, Alec, will you wait up a minute?"

"We can talk in your room, honey, while you pack up."

She stumbled on the concrete steps and he reached back, disengaging her hands and pulling her up alongside him. He kept a solicitous hand at her elbow, offering her support in her high heels. "Did you hurt yourself when you leaped out of my truck?"

"No." Nothing more than a tender ankle, and since he'd blown off the impact of a bullet wound to his thigh, she certainly wasn't going to complain about something so minor.

"Good." He continued dragging her along.

Celia seethed. She had no intention of packing up. In fact, she still had hopes of convincing Alec to stay and help her. Alec and Dane were forever claiming "gut instincts" to account for every hunch they had that couldn't be explained, but proved true nonetheless. Well, she had a wrenching, screaming "gut instinct" right now, and it was telling her that Hannah

Barrington was in big trouble and Celia was her only hope. She couldn't, wouldn't turn her back on Hannah now, no matter what. If she did give up on the twenty-year-old girl, she'd never again be able to face herself in the mirror. But she was smart enough to know her chances of actually helping Hannah would be much better if Alec lent his expertise. Getting him to do that would be tricky.

Especially if she killed him first.

When they reached the landing and circled to her room, Alec turned to face her. He reached for her purse and Celia knew a physical struggle would be pointless. He was coming in and since she hoped to convince him to help her, she didn't want to cause a fuss about it. Still, she snatched her purse out of his reach and glared at him. "I'll get the key. Just hold on a second."

He was impatient, looming over her as if he expected her to pull out a gun instead. Ha! If she had one, she would already have hit him over the head with it. Celia thrust the key into his hand and said at the same time, "I can't believe your gall. How would you like it if I broke into your home?"

He swung the door open and reached inside for a light. His voice was pitched low, with a husky drawl. "Anytime you want to visit my place, honey, you just let me know. The invitation is always open."

Celia sputtered, annoyed at what she was sure was another sexual reference. Then the light spilled over them and Alec could suddenly see into her room.

For once his look was comical rather than terrorizing. "What the hell?"

Celia peeked around his shoulder, and flinched. She'd forgotten that she'd left the room in such cluttered disarray. The room's dingy carpeting could barely be seen for the objects covering it. Alec slowly turned to stare down at her, one black brow quirked high. "What the hell have you been up to?"

"Exercising?" Her voice emerged as an embarrassed squeak. The personal goals she'd set for herself were just that—personal. She didn't want anyone, especially Alec, to know about them.

He blinked twice, his look filled with skepticism, then again surveyed her room. He took his time, his gaze going over the padded floor mat, the ankle and wrist weights, the five-pound barbells, a jump rope, and finally landing on the expandable chin-up bar she had wedged open in the bathroom doorway. So far, she'd managed to get her chin over it twice. He shook his head, and his long hair skimmed over his shoulders. "Who the hell do you think you are? That crazy broad from the Terminator movie?"

Celia's face burned and she reluctantly followed him inside, pausing beside the door. "I'm just trying to stay in shape. I was getting too soft."

His gaze caught hers and held. Two heartbeats later, he slowly reached around her and shoved the door shut with the flat of his hand. His other palm landed on the wall next to her head, caging her in. She could feel his thick wrists just touching her bare shoulders as he leaned down toward her, angling his chest so close she inhaled his scent with every rapid breath she took. "Crazy Celia," he muttered, nuzzling close to her. "I like you soft."

She thought about ducking. She thought about running. Her body had other thoughts.

When his mouth touched hers, it was like tasting live electricity. She jerked, gasping at the same time and giving him the opportunity to sink his tongue into her open mouth. Her responding groan told him things she didn't want him to know.

He ate at her mouth, big, soft, slow love bites that made her want more, made her chase his mouth with her own. She loved how he kissed. "Alec..."

"Hush, it's okay, baby." And then he gave her that killer kiss again until her arms were tight around his neck, their bodies fused together, rocking. He was so incredibly hard, so solid. She loved the way his breath was broken, how his hands shook, and the way his hips pushed rhythmically against her where she needed the pressure most...

His mouth moved to her throat, making her toes curl.

"I don't want to do this," she whispered, but where the words came from she had no idea. She hadn't been touched like this in a long time, and she wanted him so badly, her body was with him every step of the way.

Alec growled, "Yes you do."

Yes I do.

He skimmed one narrow shoulder strap down her arm while his mouth left damp, hot kisses over the sensitive skin of her collarbone, the hollow of her shoulder, the slope of her upthrust breast. She felt cool air touch her breast, then the incredible, contrasting heat of his rough palm as he slid his hand inside her bra. They both groaned together at the exquisite feel of it.

His forehead touched hers, his eyes closed as if in pain while he caressed her, gently learning the shape of her, weighing her in his palm. She could feel a subtle trembling in his entire body, could feel the harsh, rapid thumping of his heartbeat, echoing her own.

"Celia?" He continued to caress her, but his tone sounded strained, as if he held his control on a very tight, very fragile leash. He rubbed her belly with his erection, making certain she understood what he asked.

Tears threatened. Her body was screaming for her to say yes, to give in. It wouldn't take much to send her over the top, to make her mindless with release. Just the way he cupped her breast, the rough rasping of his thumb over her tender nipple, had her on the verge of climax. She felt empty and hungry, every nerve ending sizzling and alive.

And that's what upset her most of all.

Why did it have to be this way? Why was she so damn easy? She wanted to be ruled by her mind, by her caring and intelligence and pride. Not by animal lust. Alec had made it plain that he thought her incompetent, that he didn't want a relationship with her, only sex. And her body didn't care.

The sob caught her by surprise, shaming her further. Alec froze, going painfully still against her, and then he pulled his hand free and gathered her close and the emotions swelled inside her until they overflowed. She didn't want to cry on his shoulder, but as usual, he wasn't giving her any choice.

She struggled to get away from him, but his arms locked around her, not allowing so much as an inch between them.

"Shhh, it's all right." One big hand pressed to the back of her head and forced it into the notch of his shoulder. She knew her tears were wetting his bare skin; she could feel the hot, soft skin of his throat against her face. His other hand rubbed up and down the length of her spine, consoling her, comforting her, filling her with immeasurable guilt for letting things get so far out of hand.

After half a minute of fighting the inevitable she clutched him tight. It simply felt too good to be held, to be comforted. Through rough sobs and humiliating sniffles, she managed to choke out, "I don't want to want you, damn it."

He rubbed his cheek against her head and answered softly. "Yeah, I think I figured that out."

She didn't have room for much leverage, but she got a fairly decent thump of her fist against his solid chest. "Not y-y-*you*, dummy. Anyone."

His hand paused in its stroking, then picked up the soothing rhythm again. "Care to tell me why?"

"No."

"Celia." His sigh blew over her damp cheek. He tried to look at her face, but she tucked it close to him and held on tight when he tried to tilt her back. She knew her makeup was ruined and she wasn't done crying, so she had no intention of having him ogle her. "Honey, I have a hard-on that could kill, and it's not going to be going away any time soon. Don't you think it might be nice if you just explained things to me? I really would like to understand."

She shook her head.

"I know you wanted me." Again he tried to look at her, wanting confirmation, and again she resisted. "I mean, with the way you were kissing me and moving against me. And your nipples were—"

She groaned, and quickly nodded.

"Then why not, honey? We're both adults. I wouldn't hurt you, if that's what you're afraid of."

She thumped him again, indignant. "I'm not afraid of you."

She heard the smile in the way he answered. "Yes you are."

"Well, only sometimes." She sniffed once more and wiped her eyes on his T-shirt, keeping her face close so he still couldn't look at her. She wasn't ready to face anyone yet, not herself, certainly not him. "You try to make me afraid."

"No."

"Yes you do. You try to make everyone afraid."

His fingers tangled in her hair and began massaging her scalp. She still felt aroused, but now she felt sleepy, too, utterly drained and strangely protected. She hadn't cried much since finding out her fiancé was a slimeball using her to hurt her family and hoping to get rich in the bargain. She'd refused to allow herself that luxury. But crying now had felt good, sort of cathartic and cleansing. She drew a slow deep breath, and ended up hiccuping.

Alec kissed her temple. "Celia, why don't you want to make love with me?"

The way he said that made her want to throw him on the bed and do unspeakable things to his hard, gorgeous body. She started shaking again and he held her a little closer, lending his quiet support. Finally, unable to figure a way out of it, she shamefully whispered, "I'm not like most women."

That gave him pause and she could feel him thinking, coming up with so many ridiculous, off-base ideas. She shook her head. "I don't mean... I'm not physically different. Well, that is..."

"Just tell me straight out, honey. Whatever it is, we'll deal with it."

A nervous, almost hysterical giggle escaped her tight lips. Oh, she had no doubt he'd love to deal with it. Raymond certainly hadn't objected, though he'd occasionally taunted her with her weakness. After he'd been found out, Raymond had taken great pleasure in telling her how easy she'd been, how she'd offered no real challenge at all. Well, she would never be easy again, though Alec Sharpe surely did wear on her convictions.

Her mind froze up with that ugly, painful thought and she jerked away from Alec's hold, turning her back and making a zigzag, awkward path around the cluttered floor to the bathroom. She paused in the open doorway, keeping her back to him. "I want you to leave now."

Two seconds passed, and he said, "Not until you tell me what's going on."

She straightened her back and lifted her chin. He was right, after the way she'd just behaved with him, he deserved the truth. Her throat felt swollen from her recent crying jag, and her head pounded as she forced out the awful words. "I have a...a sexual problem."

Alec didn't say a word. There was such complete suffocating silence that she couldn't bear it. She darted into the bathroom and slammed the door, then leaned back against it and covered her face with her hands. Now he knew the truth. He'd likely leave in disgust, wanting nothing to do with her, and her chances of helping Hannah would diminish to almost zero. How could she help anyone else when she couldn't even help herself?

A hard pounding rattled the door, making her spring away with a short scream. She whirled, one hand clutching her heart.

"Goddammit, Celia, open this door right now!"

She stared, unable to even blink. He was angry?

The door trembled again, threatening to splinter, as Alec hammered on it. She jumped back another cautious step.

"I'm giving you to the count of two, then I'm opening the door my own way."

Celia gawked.

"One!"

He wasn't going to give her much time to consider her options, she thought. But then, there was really only one option anyway. She reached for the doorknob.

4

ALEC WAS SO MAD he could barely see straight. He opened his mouth to shout "two" and heard the lock click open. He propped his hands on his hips and narrowed his eyes, waiting for Celia to present herself. Ha, what did she think, that she could make a crazy statement like that and then just tell him to get lost? Fat chance.

He figured Raymond Stern had something to do with her little bombshell revelation, and he regretted his noble decision to let the law have him. If he could go back and do things over, he would.

"Get your butt out here, Celia."

Reluctantly she opened the door. Her face was ravaged, blotchy red from her tears and with makeup everywhere. His heart softened, making his entire system go on alert. Damn, but he would rather take a beating than see her cry. His jaw worked for a moment while he fought his natural instincts, to lift her in his arms, toss her on the bed, and prove she had not a single problem in the world. Hell, he wanted her so bad, they'd burn up the mattress in record time. And then he'd start on round two. He figured he could make love to her all night long and not get his fill. But judging by her expression, she wasn't up to a sexual marathon at the moment. Right now, she needed him rational, not ruled by an overactive libido.

He hadn't had urges this strong since he'd been a teenager, and back then, he'd had his pick of girls to handle the problem. This time, though, he didn't want anyone but Celia. And he'd wait—for just a little longer.

He drew a long breath, reaching for a modicum of control, but unwilling to let her know what a strain it was. "I want you to take a shower and change." There. That had sounded calm enough. Despite the fact that damn dress she wore was keeping his need on a razor's edge.

She nodded her head, suspiciously submissive for the moment.

"When you're done," he said, watching her closely, "we're going to talk."

"I thought you wanted to leave right away."

"Later. Maybe even in the morning. For now, just get yourself comfortable, all right?" A thought struck him and he added, "Have you eaten? Are you hungry?"

"No."

No what? No she hadn't eaten or no she wasn't hungry? He decided to make the decision himself, which was what he should have been doing all along. He'd order up some sandwiches and coffee, feed her, then get a few things settled with her.

He sighed again. "Where are your clothes?"

"In the suitcase in the closet."

She stood docile while he opened the case and

yanked out jeans and a T-shirt, then handed them to her.

"I need panties, too." She wiped at her eyes with a shaking hand, removing some of the mascara that was smudged there. His heart thumped again, and that damn tenderness threatened to bring him to his knees. Turning back to the case he grabbed up a pair of pale pink nylon panties and thrust them at her. She sniffed, turned her back, and went into the bathroom without a word.

As soon as the door clicked shut Alec thrust both hands into his hair and pulled. Christ, she was making him crazy. First fighting him tooth and nail, refusing to give so much as an inch, and now acting like an obedient child. He wasn't at all certain which he hated worse. Celia was constantly taking him off guard; he thought she probably did it on purpose just so he'd never know how to react.

He heard the water start, pictured her naked in the shower, and slammed one fist against his thigh.

To keep his mind off bare, wet, feminine skin, he called and ordered room service. Even in such a run-down rat motel, they had an attached bar with a fairly varied menu and he ordered two sub sandwiches, a pot of coffee and pie. While he was waiting for that to be delivered, he called Dane.

The line was answered on the second ring.

"Yeah?"

Alec heard feminine giggling in the background. He should have known, given the time of night, Dane would be preoccupied. He rolled his eyes. Dane's marital bliss was about enough to choke a lesser man, but Alec could take it—barely. "I found your sister."

He heard a shuffling, and the next words were muffled. "Shh, just a minute honey. It's Alec." Then into the receiver, "Good job. I never doubted it, Alec. Now I'm kind of busy—"

"She was dressed like a tramp, hanging out in a bar trying to pick up Jacobs."

Dane uttered one short, crude word.

"Yeah, that's how I figured it. I got her out of there, but she's determined to go back. She has some damned vigilante attitude about saving Hannah Barrington." Alec couldn't quite keep the disgust from his tone, but every time he thought of Celia putting herself on the line for the Barrington girl he wanted to rage against the injustice of it.

Very quietly, Dane said, "I'm glad she's concerned, despite how you feel about it, Alec. But I don't want her involved in that mess."

"I threatened to fire her if she didn't back off."

Dane cursed again.

With a wry twist to his mouth, Alec said, "I see you already guessed how she reacted to that."

"You're slipping, buddy."

"Like hell. I'll drag her home if I have to. But I'm not leaving her here alone to tangle with Jacobs."

"Why are you so worried if you really think there's no problem for Hannah?"

Alec stilled as he realized he'd backed himself into a corner. Even Dane didn't know his complete reasoning for wanting no part of this particular case, but being Dane, he was likely making some pretty damn astute guesses. Alec tried for a bluff. "Hannah's probably having the time of her life. But your damn sister alone is trouble waiting to happen."

"Celia's not as fragile as you think." Alec heard a voice in the background, heard Dane whispering, and then he said, "Angel wants to talk to you."

"No! Damn it, Dane, don't you dare—"

"Hello, Alec."

Alec sighed. When he got Dane alone, he was going to strangle him. "Hi, hon. How're you feeling?" Angel didn't seem to have any problems carrying this baby, but like Dane, Alec would feel a lot better if she took things a little easier. The trauma she'd gone through with her first son, Grayson, was still fresh in everyone's mind—except maybe Angel's.

"I'd be feeling a lot better if you'd quit trying to bully Celia."

"Well—"

"I've gotten rather fond of you, Alec, despite my first impressions. And Grayson adores you. But if you don't stop pushing Celia around, she's going to kill you."

"Well—"

"Not only that, but I'd think you could be a little more understanding. She's trying to start a new life, which means putting the old life behind her. But you won't help her at all! All you keep doing is telling her that she can't possibly do it."

"Well—"

"I've finally gotten Dane to lighten up on her a little, and what do you do? You step in and pretend to be her father and big brother and husband all wrapped into one."

Alec held the phone away from his head and stared at it, appalled. He sure as hell didn't feel like a blood relative where Celia was concerned, and he'd be damned if he'd ever be a husband again. He was a man who learned from life's little lessons, and that one in particular was one he'd never forget.

When he cautiously returned the receiver to his ear, he caught Angel in mid-tirade, still going strong. The water shut off in the bathroom and Alec quickly interrupted Angel. "I gotta go, sweetie. Tell Dane not to worry. I'll take care of things."

"Wait a minute!"

He sighed again, feeling very put upon. "What?"

Angel wasn't the least put off by his surly tone. "Will you stay there and help Celia or not?"

Tonight appeared to be his night to reason with unreasonable women. "It's dangerous, Angel. She could get hurt."

"Not with you there to watch over things. Dane says you're the very best. I know you can handle this and make sure Celia stays safe."

He felt cornered, damn it, and his tone lowered to a growl. "I don't *want* to stay here and make sure she's safe. It's a wasted trip."

"Celia doesn't think so."

The soft way Angel spoke made him feel guilty. Was he being insensitive to Celia? Was it really so dangerous that he couldn't indulge her, or was it just his own personal prejudice against this case that was deciding him?

It took him less than two seconds to realize it was both.

Angel wasn't done laying on the guilt. Funny how all women seemed to instinctively know the shortest route to manipulating a man, even a man they couldn't claim as their own.

Why the hell didn't Dane step in and provide some distraction?

"Alec, are you listening to me?"

"Yeah."

"If you're not going to stay, then I can't possibly go off on a trip and leave Celia alone. She'll need someone who understands and supports her."

Alec wondered if offering understanding and support would soften Celia a little, help remove that damn "no" from her vocabulary.

Dane's hard tone interrupted his musing, blaring into the phone even though Angel still held it. *"He'll stay."*

Giving in to the inevitable, now that he'd admitted to himself he *could* keep Celia safe, Alec echoed with a sigh, "I'll stay."

"Good." There was a second's pause, just enough to prepare him, before she added, "We love you, Alec."

He heard Dane snicker in the background and felt his entire face heat. He hated it when Angel did that, got all mushy on him, and Dane damn well knew it, which was probably why he encouraged her in that melodramatic crap. He didn't want her to say the words and he sure as hell didn't want her to feel them. Not for him. He could do without love, just as he always had. In fact, he preferred it that way.

Of course, what he preferred never seemed to matter much once Angel had her mind set on something. And she'd made him a part of their family, which meant she was determined that he accept her love. Unaccountable female.

Trying not to sound too surly, or worse, like he was embarrassed by her affection, Alec muttered, "Yeah, well, good night." He hung up quickly, just as Celia opened the bathroom door and stepped out.

She had on faded jeans that fit her slim legs to perfection and a soft, thin T-shirt that draped over the small mounds of her breasts. She looked great dressed up, but he found her just as appealing when she dressed down, maybe even more so.

The first thing that clearly registered in his beleaguered brain was the fact she was braless. Then he took in her bare feet, her scrubbed pink face and slicked-back, still-wet hair, and everything in him tightened. Brother, father, husband hell. He wanted to be her lover.

He stood slowly, unable to pull his gaze away from her. "I ordered up some food. It should be here soon."

She nodded, not quite meeting his eyes. She had that killer dress and the high heels in her arms and she laid them aside on the dresser. As she moved, Alec noticed her limping slightly and he scowled.

"Are you hurt?"

"No."

He stepped closer, just about sick of her playing so

timid. On some level, he enjoyed scrapping with her, though he'd never admit it to her. But fighting with Celia was, in many ways, more enjoyable than having sex with other women. It surely heated his blood more. Of course, everything to do with Celia heated his blood.

He caught her chin and lifted it. "Don't ever lie to me, Celia. You're limping. Did you hurt yourself when you jumped out of my truck?"

Her lashes were still spiky from the shower. She blinked slowly, her hazel eyes bright, and a slight flush pinkened her skin. "My feet are sore. I'm not used to wearing high heels anymore."

He moved his thumb, gently brushing it back and forth over her small rounded chin. Her skin was so soft, he wanted to touch her all over, rub himself naked against her, feel that softness under him, accepting him. He took a steadying breath. "I'll rub your feet for you."

Her eyes widened and she nervously blurted, "I want to make a deal with you."

One brow lifted high. He was about to tell her he'd stay and help her with the damn Barrington case, just so she could relax and stop being so jumpy, but now she had him curious. He led her over to the edge of the bed, urged her to sit, then knelt before her. He lifted one small foot into his hands, and as he started rubbing, pressing his thumbs into her arch, he said, "So? What's the deal?" Her toes curled in his hand, making him smile.

"I need your help if I'm going to be able to do any good with this case."

"Yes, you do." He flexed her foot, heard her small groan and began rubbing each small, pink toe. She had nice feet, as intrinsically female as the rest of her. They were so small, so narrow and smooth and pale, they seemed swallowed up by his large rough hands.

"I'll...I'll do anything you want if you'll help me save Hannah."

His hands stilled. His gaze shot from her foot to her face and narrowed there. He didn't say anything, not trusting himself to speak.

Celia appeared to be holding her breath, her eyes round, the pulse in the hollow of her throat fluttering anxiously. When he only watched her, doing his best to keep his anger under wraps, she burst out in nervous explanation. "I know you think I'm not fit to do this work. You've done nothing but harp on me about quitting, about going back to the family business." She paused, drew a deep breath. "Well, I'll do it."

"It?" He couldn't get his jaw to work, so the one-word question was whispered through clenched teeth.

She nodded. "I'll...I'll go back. But only if you help me to help Hannah first."

The tension eased out of him by slow degrees. She wasn't bartering her body as he'd first assumed. She'd agree to quit, to return to her old job where she'd be safe. It was what he'd wanted, what he knew would be best for her. Angel's words echoed in his mind, making his muscles tense with guilt. *She'll need someone who understands and supports her.* Very slowly, he released her foot and put both hands on her knees.

Still holding her gaze, he gently urged her legs apart. Whatever Celia needed, he wanted to give it to her.

Her eyes widened again, but he was already there, already moving up over her, gently easing her down onto the mattress while wedging himself firmly between her soft, spread thighs. He closed his eyes, relishing the feel of her beneath him, the gentle cradle of her open body. Pressing his hips down and in, he moved against her, torturing himself with the pleasure of it.

"Alec?" Her voice was high and thin.

"What if that's not what I want the most, Celia?" He felt his heart drumming, his stomach twisting with need. "What then?"

She swallowed hard, the sound audible in the quiet room. She blinked twice before squarely meeting his gaze. "I can't give up on Hannah."

His senses ignited, heat rushing over him in waves. All he could think was that she was giving in to him, she wanted him to make love to her.

He leaned down to kiss her, already breathless with anticipation—and a knock sounded on the door.

His head jerked up and his entire body went rigid as he instinctively prepared for the possible threat.

"Room service!"

Several curses came to mind, but it was Celia scrambling out from beneath him, her panic almost tangible as she leapt from the bed and rushed back into the bathroom, that helped him maintain control. Once again, that door was slammed.

Alec flopped down on the bed and flung one arm over his eyes. Tonight wasn't going at all as planned.

And given what had just almost happened, he had a feeling it was going to get a lot worse before it got better. Typical, whenever he dealt with Celia.

CELIA SLOWLY CHEWED on her sandwich. She didn't really want it, not when nothing had been settled between them. She felt like an idiot for fleeing to the bathroom again. At least this time Alec hadn't abused the door to get her out. He'd merely asked her if she was ready to eat, and she'd calmly walked out as if she hadn't been hiding. Dumb. She had to get a grip if she wanted to talk him into helping her.

The noisy air conditioner in her room barely took the edge off the heat. The air felt heavy, thick. The food tasted bland to her nervous tongue. Alec sat across from her at the small, scarred table wedged into the corner of the room. There was barely space to move between it and the edge of the bed. He'd sat so that he faced the door, a conscious decision on his part because Alec was always alert, always prepared. With him, she had no doubt she could save Hannah.

But Alec kept looking at her with his narrow-eyed gaze, speculating, just waiting to start grilling her and putting her on the spot. She decided to beat him to the punch. The key to dealing with Alec was to stay in control.

She cleared her throat, took a large swallow of the coffee, then looked him dead in the eye.

Sheesh, he was gorgeous.

"Come on, honey, out with it." Alec grinned slightly, one eyebrow lifted. "I can see you have something to say, so say it."

Celia scowled. "How do you do that?"

"Read your mind?" He tugged at his earring absently. "I don't know, except that we've got some kind of chemistry going, whether you want to admit it or not."

She lowered her eyes. "Actually, that's part of my...um, problem."

"Your *sexual* problem?"

Heat rushed into her cheeks. She hated the way he just blurted that out, but she knew he was deliberately rattling her, so she lifted her chin and again forced herself to meet his gaze. "Yes."

Alec took a healthy bite of his own sandwich, taking his time while he chewed and swallowed. "Didn't seem to me like you had a problem." His attention dropped to her breasts and her nipples immediately peaked. His eyes narrowed. "Everything appears to be working just fine."

She had to lock her knees to keep from running away again. She was so ashamed of herself, it was all she could do to sit there and face him. "That's part of the problem."

Now he looked surprised, and a tad annoyed. He swallowed the last of his food and glared. "Come again?"

Fiddling with the spoon for her coffee just to give her fingers something to do, Celia admitted, "I'm not very discriminating. I suppose I'm what's called a loose woman." She felt his gaze like a laser burn and this time she couldn't look up.

"A loose woman?"

Something in his tone sounded lethal and she

braced herself. "After the way I let Raymond use me, putting so many people in danger, I decided I would never again get involved with a man who didn't really care about me. I thought I had learned my lesson, that my pride was enough to keep me from being foolish. But..." She swallowed hard, searching for the right words. "You...you look at me, and I forget all my convictions."

"This is all because you *want* me?" He sounded irritated and a little disbelieving.

"I want you. But not for the right reasons."

Alec shot out of his chair and she braced herself, watching him wide-eyed. Rather than come to her, he stalked away, his hands on his hips, his shoulders rigid. Through the tight T-shirt, she could clearly see every muscle of his back.

"Alec, when we first met you made it clear you didn't want a relationship. Every time we're together you make it clear that you don't trust me, that you don't even really like me."

He whipped around to stare at her, incredulous.

She faltered just a bit, but her gut instincts toward Hannah couldn't be ignored. "You just want me for sex, and as much as my body might like the idea, my brain is disgusted and ashamed."

"Your brain?" He started toward her, slowly stalking, his eyes narrowed and intent on her face.

She quickly slid out of her chair and stepped behind it. The crowded room gave her little enough space to navigate. "Stop trying to intimidate me! I hate it when you do that, especially when I'm only trying to give you the truth."

"The truth being that you have some harebrained idea that sex without love everlasting is dirty?"

He stopped in front of her, towering, angry. Celia pushed the chair aside and pointed her finger at him, her own anger taking over. "Sex without some kind of emotional commitment is dirty! It's just sex."

"Which can be damn satisfying!"

"Not for me!" She realized they were both screaming and tried to calm herself. Good grief, she didn't want to run him off, and she certainly didn't want everyone in the motel to know their personal business. She pushed a hand through her wet hair and took several deep breaths. "I'm sorry for sort of leading you on. You kiss me, and I forget what I'm doing and what it is I want to do. I'd appreciate it if you wouldn't touch me anymore."

"Like hell."

Celia ignored that. "I have a lot to make up for, Alec, mostly because I was blinded by Raymond and who he was. And the reason I was so blinded—"

"I don't want to hear this, damn it."

"Is because sex between us was—" She almost choked, then forced the words out. "It was great."

"*Goddammit.*" Alec's hand grabbed her arms and pulled her up on tiptoe. "Celia—"

Whatever he was going to say was cut off by the loud beeping of her pager. They both froze for a moment, and Alec seemed to be vibrating with anger, struggling for control. Celia waited, practically hanging in his grip, though strangely not worried. For whatever reason, this time she didn't fear him. Alec would never hurt her, and she knew it.

He slowly released her until her feet touched flat on the floor. She rushed over to the dresser where her beeper lay. She hadn't taken it with her to the bar, too afraid it would go off and Jacobs would discover something that would give her away. She picked it up and read the number blinking at her with a distinct feeling of dread.

Biting her lip, she turned to face Alec.

"Who is it?" He had himself under control, but it was a tenuous hold. Everything he felt was still there in his glittering black eyes, plain for her to see. From the inside out, she felt the trembling start.

Watching him closely, she said, "It's...Mrs. Barrington."

Alec turned away, but Celia was already rushing to him, personal reservations forgotten in the face of Hannah's need. "Alec?" When he didn't answer she shifted around so she was in front of him and he had no choice but to listen to her. "Please, I need your help with this case. Hannah needs your help." She ignored his snort of disbelief and continued. "I have to call her back. Alec? *Please*, will you stay and help me?"

He stared at the ceiling for a good full minute, not answering. Celia could feel his indecision and she held herself still, allowing him to decide while at the same time hoping against hope that he wouldn't turn her down.

Finally he looked at her, and she'd never seen him harder, more determined. Her heartbeat shuddered, then began a rapid tattoo.

"Yeah, Celia, I'll stay. I'll help you save little Hannah Barrington, whether the girl wants saving or not." He looked her over, his gaze more cold than hot now. "But there's a condition."

Despite his cynical, detached attitude, a warmth spread through her, proof of what she'd already guessed, what she'd always known, exactly what he'd want in return. Her legs felt shaky, but she lifted her chin and returned his direct stare, bravado her only defense. "I'm listening."

His eyelids drooped sensually, his thick lashes almost hiding his gaze as he stared at first her mouth, then her breasts, then lower. His tone was soft, a raw growl that made her every nerve ending tingle with awareness. "I want you. Whenever and wherever I decide. Any way I choose to take you—" His gaze lifted, meeting hers again. "—and I'll choose a hell of a lot of ways. You'll say yes. Until this is over, until Hannah is on her way home, you'll be mine."

Celia rolled her lips in to contain a moan, unable to look away, unable to say a single word. Damn, but she was almost relieved. He was going to take the decision out of her hands, and her belly curled in anticipation even as she feared her own response.

Alec smirked, the gesture sensual and ripe with promise. "Oh no, honey," he whispered, "I'm not going to let you play at being a martyr. I'm going to make damn sure you enjoy every little thing I do to you, with no holding back. Whatever the hell you did with Raymond won't be able to compare. And when I'm done, you'll know damn good and well that nothing between us is dirty."

His hands cupped her hot cheeks and turned her

face up to his. "You can call Mrs. Barrington and tell her not to worry, that everything will be taken care of." His thumb brushed her bottom lip, hot and rough. "And then you can strip those jeans off and get into bed."

She gasped.

"Or you can tell me to go to hell." His eyes glittered, bright with intent. "The decision is yours."

Celia licked her dry lips, trying to find words around the wild racing of her heart. He hadn't even really touched her yet and she felt ready to lose control. How would she ever survive? Did she have any choice?

"I'll...I'll call Mrs. Barrington."

His eyes blazed with sudden heat at her acceptance, his nostrils flaring in excitement, like a wild animal sensing victory. For just a heartbeat his hands tightened and she thought her time of reckoning was at hand, that he'd lost control. Then he stepped away. "I have to get a few things out of my truck. I can stay with you tonight, because everyone expected it. But tomorrow I'll have to get my own room just in case anyone has the sense to check up on you."

Celia stood mute, watching him.

"Go ahead and make your call. In the morning, I'll figure how out we're going to handle things."

She watched him leave the room, his body moving with fluid grace and blatant strength. She didn't bother asking what they'd do tonight. She already knew.

She drew in a shuddering breath, tamped down on her guilt and shame while telling herself she was only doing what was necessary. Then she reached for the phone. She didn't want to be occupied when Alec returned; she didn't want to have to disrobe in front of him.

She'd be in the bed, hiding under the covers.

Everything else was up to him.

5

ALEC LINGERED in the parking lot for several reasons.

First and foremost, he had to get control of himself. Holding out a hand, he stared in disgust at the trembling in his own body, a body usually so cold nothing affected it, certainly not a woman. For years, too many to count, he'd been able to take pleasure in a woman's body, to give pleasure back, without letting it get to him.

He felt damn affected now, and he hadn't even really touched the little witch. Heaven help him when he got himself buried deep inside her, when he felt the hot wet clasp of her body, heard her half-frightened, mostly excited moans...

Cursing, he paced furiously around his truck, trying to outrun the truth of his feelings. She did fear him a little, and for now, nothing would change that. He didn't even want to change it because although he made her nervous, she still wanted him, almost as much as he wanted her. He knew having sex with Celia would blow his mind out, and the knowing was almost worse than the actual effects. Like a drug he knew could destroy him, he wanted her anyway. Being as cold and indifferent as possible was his only defense.

But when she looked up at him with those innocent

hazel eyes, he wanted to protect her, even from himself. And that was another reason he hesitated.

He should have killed Raymond; killing him would make Alec feel a whole lot better now. *She'd said sex between them had been great.* He squeezed his eyes shut and considered howling at the moon. The words, and her tortured look that had accompanied them, filled him with such a killing rage, he knew he'd have to do whatever he could to erase that bastard from her body, from her soul. If she didn't thank him in the beginning, she would by the end. He had to believe that.

Knowing he'd stalled long enough, that Celia could well be trying to sneak out the tiny bathroom window, he grabbed his gear from his truck and headed back in. Every muscle in his body felt tight and strained, his jaw locked, his mind in turmoil. The hard-on he'd learned to associate with any close proximity to Celia throbbed insistently. He hated needing her like this. He hated to need anyone.

Half expecting the door to be locked now, he was taken aback when it swung open easily and he found Celia lying wide-eyed in the narrow bed—very obviously naked beneath all the blankets.

The covers were pulled so high, even her chin was hidden, with her rounded eyes looking almost comical over the hem. Twin sets of slender fingers gripped the blankets on either side of her mouth. A strange feeling, like mingled tenderness and raging lust, rushed through him, making him light-headed, almost dizzy with triumph and hunger. He liked seeing her in a bed, waiting for *him*. Oh yeah, he liked it a lot. Too damn much.

His mouth kicked up in a crooked smile as he dropped his overnight bag on the floor and put his pistol on the bedside table. Celia's eyes rounded even more at the sight of the weapon.

"You carry a...a gun?"

He gave her a level look, amazed at her naiveté. "All the agents do, Celia."

"I don't... That is...should I?"

Alec shook his head, astounded that a feeling as light as amusement could touch him now when he could feel the furious drumming of his heart. "Hell no. One leg wound is enough for me."

"*I* didn't shoot you!"

He started to sit on the side of the bed, then thought better of it. If he got that close, all his plans would end before they could begin. He wasn't ready yet. He needed at least a few more minutes to shore up his determination.

He stepped back a few paces and leaned on the wall, watching her. "I can think of a dozen times in the last few hours when you might have."

"Well..." She considered that, then shrugged in resignation. "Yeah."

His gaze sharpened and he deliberately used a tone he knew drew attention from hired killers. "You don't need a weapon, sweetheart, because after this, you won't be taking any more dangerous cases."

Her fingers tightened on the blankets and her eyes narrowed. But thankfully, for his peace of mind, she kept silent.

Still holding her gaze, Alec reached down and un-buckled his belt. Celia blinked hard, her gaze skim-ming down his body then immediately shooting back up again in a visibly desperate bid to stay on his face. With a whistling sound, the leather belt slid out of the jean loops and he draped it over the back of a chair.

"Alec?" Her voice was a squeak, anxious and em-barrassed and if he was any judge, turned-on. "What are we going to do about Hannah? Do you have a plan?"

He pulled his shirt over his head and heard her soft groan. "I have several plans, sweetheart. Why don't we talk about my plan for tonight, for right now?" After tossing the shirt aside he scratched his bare chest and saw her fascinated gaze. Very softly, he asked, "You want details?"

"No...yes...*no.*"

He grinned. "Indecisive, aren't we? Well, I think I want to tell you anyway."

"Alec, I think—"

"You think sex is dirty, I know."

She squeezed her eyes closed and for a brief cow-ardly moment pulled the blankets over her head. Sec-onds later she jerked it down again to stare at him.

Celia was no coward.

"Okay." She drew a deep fortifying breath. "What are you going to do, Alec?"

She had to be smothering under all those blankets. The cheap motel had inadequate air, and though the air conditioner rattled and hummed loudly, it couldn't keep up with the oppressive July heat. Alec had already begun to sweat, but then, that had a lot to do with Celia being so close and naked.

Toeing off his low boots then bending to remove his socks, he said, "I'm going to let you get familiar with my body."

"Oh..."

Hearing the trembling in her tone nearly did him in. He'd always considered himself a strong man; physically he knew it was true, but mentally, emotionally, she had him concerned. He couldn't think of a single challenge he'd ever backed away from, and he always accepted knowing he'd win, his confidence never wavering. But he didn't know if he was strong enough to do this tonight. He hoped so, because Miss Celia Carter was in desperate need of a few lessons, and damned if he'd let any other man give them to her.

Number one, the most important lesson, that he wasn't Raymond and other than gender, had not a single thing in common with that scum.

But just telling her that wouldn't do it. And neither would having sex with her when she was so skittish and unsure of herself. Oh, she'd take him, all right. He had no doubts on that score. She'd take him and enjoy herself immensely. Used to be, that would have been enough for him. But not now.

He wanted her to openly want him, to admit it was right between them. To accept that sometimes sex was just plain meant to be and this was one of those times. There was no shame in that.

If he took her now, she'd be ashamed.

Damn. Alec cursed to himself, but couldn't find any

way around that truth. Celia fought against her natural instincts. He'd never seen a woman so responsive, so easily aroused as his Celia. It was a gift, one he planned to enjoy and wanted her to appreciate.

So he planned to teach her, slowly, to accept him and what they could have together for as long as the chemistry lasted. She'd learn, little by little, and he had no doubt he'd die by small degrees with each lesson.

He unbuttoned his fly and slid down the zipper, carefully because he was so fully erect he ached like never before. The soft, hungry moan Celia gave told him eventually he'd have his reward. The torture would be worth it.

"Don't close your eyes, Celia."

Her hands covered her face.

"Celia, look at me." His command was soft, insistent.

She shook her head. "Alec, I can't. I..." Her voice emerged breathy, so aroused she aroused him just by speaking.

"You have no choice, sweetheart, remember?" He pushed the jeans down, taking his dark briefs with them, and stepped away from his clothing. Celia's naked shoulders were now visible and he wanted to start kissing her there, eating her there, then working his way down until he'd devoured every hidden, hot inch of her. He drew a deep breath.

When he was right next to the bed, so close his naked thigh nearly touched the mattress, he said, "Look at me, Celia."

She jumped, startled by his approach. His silent

movements often had that effect on people; even Dane had commented on his stealth, cursing him on occasion for taking him unawares.

With her bottom lip firmly caught between her teeth, she slowly lifted her lashes. Heat rushed into her cheeks and her breasts trembled with small, rapid breaths, making the covers flutter.

Alec studied her, forcing himself to stick to his plan despite the gripping need to take her. "Does my body look dirty to you, Celia?"

Gaze glued to his erection, she shook her head no.

He put one knee on the bed and she rolled slightly toward him, her expression almost panicked.

"Shhh. Don't get jumpy on me." He caught the edge of the blankets and they went through a silent tug-of-war before Celia closed her eyes again and released them.

Very slowly, feeling every punch of his heartbeat as it resounded through his body, Alec bared her. He threw the covers completely off the bed. For now at least, they wouldn't need them.

Stiff, nearly frozen, her only movement that of her choked breaths, she remained obediently quiet while Alec visually explored her. Her small rounded breasts were perfect, flushed a warm pink, softly upright, shimmering with her nervousness and excitement. Her nipples were drawn achingly tight, dark rose, and more than anything he wanted them in his mouth, wanted to suck on her and hear her small cries. He swallowed hard and continued his visual feast.

Her skin, pale and so smooth, would chafe easily

beneath his whiskers, and he mentally cautioned himself to be careful. Her navel made a slight, tempting dent in her softly rounded belly, and below that...

His nostrils expanded on a sharp breath. Dark blond curls covered her in a small neat triangle. Without his mind's permission, his hand lifted and he covered her, then he groaned softly. Celia jerked, a shocked, highly erotic sound coming from deep in her throat.

"Look, Celia," he urged her. She shook her head and his fingers tightened. "Look at how my hand covers you completely. I can feel the heat pulsing off you." He leaned down and nuzzled her belly, nearly incoherent with lust. "And I can smell your scent. You're every damn bit as turned on as I am."

Panting, she whispered, "Alec?"

He realized she was close, that in only those few moments with nothing more than a scattering of words and a possessive touch, she was nearing the edge. *She was incredible.* In a voice he barely recognized as his own, Alec murmured, "I like seeing you, honey. There sure as hell isn't anything dirty about you."

The sound she made drew his attention back to her face and the sight of her nearly ecstatic pain helped him regain control. He raised his hand to her cheek, then slowly smoothed her mouth, urging her to release her lip from the grip of her teeth. "Don't hurt yourself, baby. Everything's okay."

Tears leaked from beneath her lashes and with a quavery voice she said, "I'm so...so easy."

Alec lay down beside her, no longer needing an incentive to keep himself under control. Her pain had done that for him. He drew her naked body close and above the lust he felt the overwhelming need to protect, to reassure, to comfort. For now at least, she was his woman, and he'd move heaven and earth to keep her from being hurt, even from herself.

"You're special, Celia, a gift to any man lucky enough to grab your attention." Very deliberately, his hand slid down her belly again. He couldn't let her stay like this, not when he knew damn well he could ease her.

Her hips immediately thrust against his searching fingers and she groaned, gripping him tight. "Alec, *please kiss me...*"

He did, devouring her mouth, searching with his tongue as he searched with his fingers.

Her flesh was so soft, so slick with eagerness. His fingers glided, probed, found the friction and rhythm that made her instantly wild. She wriggled against him, deliberately arousing herself further by moving her nipples over his chest, sucking on his tongue. She was hot and carnal and—oh hell—she was his.

Within two minutes she was coming apart in his arms and Alec cursed even as he fought to hold his own reaction at bay. Losing control, releasing himself on her belly, wouldn't do a damn thing toward convincing her that sex was good and wholesome, not something to hide away from.

She bit him, his mouth, his chin, then his shoulder, and her nails dug deep into the muscles of his back, the small stings helping him keep control. When she slumped, sweaty and hot and limp in his arms, Alec kissed her forehead and smoothed her hair back.

"That was a long time coming."

She didn't answer, apparently too dazed to form words.

"Celia, if you act embarrassed or ashamed, I swear I'll turn you over my knee."

She lightly bit him again, this time on his muscled chest. "Don't forget your gun is still close, Sharpe. I'm not afraid to use it."

Grinning, while doing his best to ignore his own pounding need, Alec reached to the floor and snagged the top sheet. Tucking her up against his side, he said, "You're going to sleep right here, against my body, all night, honey. Don't even think of moving away. You got that?"

Her brows lowered as her eyes opened and she stared up at him. "But...sleep? What about—"

He cupped her cheek and kissed her nose. "We're not finishing this little game until you ask me, very nicely, to do so."

She searched his face and he could detect her mental shrug. "All right, I—"

He laid a finger against her lips. "Not now, Celia. Not when you're still all soft from a nice climax." Her cheeks turned bright pink at his frank talk and he smiled. "You'll know when you're ready, when you want me without all this ridiculous reserve. Then I'll take you until neither of us can walk. I promise. But for tonight, we sleep."

He reached over and switched off the light, then gathered her close again. Her thighs cradled his erection, making him grit his teeth. After several silent moments, she whispered, "I won't make it easy on you, Alec."

He shook his head. "You never have, babe."

CELIA WOKE with her nose pressed to a hard, very warm, somewhat hairy chest. She smiled, snuggling closer and deeply inhaling the delicious scent of warm male flesh, but within the space of a single heartbeat she remembered Alec and what he'd done and what she'd done... Oh no. She opened her eyes slowly and like a zombie, lifted her head to survey him.

Breathing deeply in his sleep, more at peace than she'd ever seen him, he looked sexier than any man she'd known. He had one long, muscled arm beneath her neck and around her back, keeping her pressed to his body. His other arm was bent up behind his head, opening his body to her perusal, making him look somewhat vulnerable. She could see the dark tuft of fine hair beneath his arm, the way his biceps bulged even when relaxed. His long silky hair was tousled, lying over his brow and touching his wide shoulders. The single gold earring shone dully in the morning light.

His jaw and chin were very dark with beard shadow, and she knew when he awakened, he'd look more menacing than ever. But for now, his long sooty lashes rested on his high cheekbones, presenting elongated shadows in the dim room, and he looked entirely too...*cuddly*.

Saying he was beautiful would have been an extreme understatement.

A soft sigh escaped her and she felt her heart lurch. Given a choice, she would have cuddled down next to him and gone blissfully back to sleep. But she knew Alec, knew his way, and understood that she couldn't let her guard down around him for a minute. Being the natural predator, he'd take swift advantage of any opening she gave him.

Not that she hadn't already given him plenty, she thought, feeling her face go hot with the memory of the past night. But she wouldn't let him win. He hoped to intimidate her enough to make her head home, leaving poor Hannah abandoned.

That would explain why he'd toyed with her so deliciously without actually taking her. She shivered, aware of him on every level. But while she physically appreciated his finesse, she didn't like his motives. If he wanted to be a caveman, she couldn't fight him, but neither did she dare give in to him completely.

Raymond had hurt her pride, but Alec could kill it.

He shifted in his sleep and her eyes were drawn to his body. The blankets only covered him as high as his navel, leaving a lot of incredible skin still bare. He was naturally dark, determinedly hard, and as much man as any woman could ever hope for.

She looked back up at the broad expanse of his solid shoulders, then gasped. High on his shoulder was a bruise, a bruise she knew had been caused by her teeth.

Last night, when the pleasure had taken her, she'd bitten him.

Her reaction was swift, the bitter reality cutting her deep and forcing her to stifle an instinctive cry of pain. She started to scramble upward, wanting to escape the proof of her own unrestrained tendencies, but suddenly found herself flat on her back. Alec, the cad, was wide awake.

"Where do you think you're going?" His voice was rough velvet, still heavy with sleep, but his eyes were sharply alert.

"Let me go, Alec."

He searched her face, his dark gaze almost obsidian in the vague morning light. She could see him thinking, calculating, and it enraged her. Pushing against his chest with all her might, she said through her teeth, "*Let—me—go.*"

Her struggles had no effect on him. She may as well have been fighting solid granite. "You were looking me over, getting used to my body. Why the sudden panic?"

Celia froze. Had he been awake the whole time? Been aware of her scrutiny? "I did not panic."

"No? What would you call it?" Before she could answer, he added in a low rumble, "Damn woman, but you look hot first thing in the morning." And then he kissed her.

Celia tried to resist him, she really did. But he smelled manly and warm and his mouth had a slightly musky taste to it from sleep. His whiskers rasped her cheek as he deepened the kiss, his hands coming up to roughly cradle her breasts. She arched into him, unable to help herself.

And he lifted away. His lips still touching hers, he said, "Now tell me what's wrong."

Her gaze didn't seem to want to focus and her heart was working way too hard for first thing in the morning. "I...I need coffee."

"As soon as you talk to me."

Damn stubborn man. He wouldn't give up, so she had to. Resolving the problem and getting out of the bed, out from under him, was a major priority. Lowering her lashes because she really couldn't look at him while making such an admission, she said in a small voice, "I bit you."

She could hear his grin, felt the renewed caressing of her breasts, gentle and easy. "Several times."

"No, I mean..." She peeked up at him, trying to gather her wits. *Several times?* Oh good grief, it just kept getting worse and worse. She felt almost sick with dread and tried to order her thoughts, but it was extremely difficult with him lying on her, all hard muscle and hot male.

She drew a slow breath. "You have a...a bruise on your shoulder."

He looked over at his shoulder, then dismissed the small mark with a shrug. "So?"

Her bottom lip trembled and she tightened her mouth to still the small giveaway. "I'm sorry."

"Sorry for being sexy? For having an incredibly healthy sex drive? Hell, woman, I *liked* it, okay? That little nibble says you were feeling everything just as I wanted you to feel it. Just as you're supposed to feel it."

"*No.*" She wouldn't let him make light of it, not

when she knew different. "I hurt you, Alec. I behaved no better than a...an animal."

His eyes darkened more, then he nuzzled her neck just below her ear. "You had a really nice orgasm, honey, full-blown, just as I wanted you to. I liked it. If you acted like an animal, then so did I, because that little love nibble all but pushed me over the edge, and knowing the reason for it damn sure made me feel pretty terrific." He kissed her earlobe, and his warm, damp tongue tickled over the rim of her ear, making her breath catch. And then he was looking at her again, waiting for her to accept what he'd said.

Heart racing, she thought about it, and pondered her own naiveté in sexual matters. Despite her limited experience, she asked, "Do you...?"

"What?" His slow smile came again. "Bite?"

The humor and hunger and tenderness in his black eyes made her stomach feel empty and her skin feel hot. But the room was dim and quiet, the day still early. Asking intimate questions seemed as perfectly timed as possible. "Yes."

His lids lowered sensually and he moved his mouth to the place where her shoulder and neck met. Celia shivered, then quickly braced herself when she felt his mouth open, felt the touch of his teeth. He did bite, but it didn't hurt. Just the opposite. The bite was wet and soft and he immediately soothed it with his tongue, making her nerves tingle.

"I would never do anything to hurt you."

Her eyes drifted shut. "Alec..."

He scooted downward in the bed, kicking the sheet away and situating himself comfortably. His mouth

stayed on her, taking small delicious nibbles all along
the way until he reached the tip of her breast. Her
heart thundered so that she wondered why it didn't
explode. He prepared her, plumping her breast,
smoothing the nipple with his calloused thumb until
it stiffened and stood turgid beneath his attention.
Every nerve in her body seemed suspended, waiting.
Then he nipped her.

Celia jumped, groaning at the same time when
Alec held her firmly in place. He did it again and
again, sometimes plucking with his lips, sometimes
tugging with his teeth. It was an erotic mixture of
foreplay; taut expectancy—though no real injury ever
came—and sinful teasing. Her toes curled under the
sheet, her hands fisted in his soft, cool hair.

The man was cruel, playing with her for long
minutes and when she did finally think he was
through, he only switched to the other breast. When
she moaned out a protest, he mumbled something
about breakfast and continued. Celia curled her legs
around him and squeezed. That didn't help, so she
pushed herself against him and Alec helped by curv-
ing one large hand over her derriere and urging her
into a slow, hypnotic rhythm against his body.

She'd thought herself fully experienced, even jaded
after her time with Raymond, but she'd never done
anything like this, or anything like last night. Alec
was either the most inventive lover in the world, or
her experiences with Raymond hadn't been adequate
to prepare her for Alec.

She tended to believe it was a mix of the two. Especially when she felt herself on the verge of a climax.

Alec seemed to sense it, too. He lifted his head, staring at her hard, his jaw working as if he felt undecided.

His eyes narrowed, and very slowly, he pushed her back away from him. Her heart broke and she wanted to cry out in shame and disappointment, but he didn't give her a chance. He grasped her hips and leaned down, then nuzzled his face into her belly.

Celia was genuinely shocked. He wasn't leaving her, he was... "*Alec.*"

He held her firmly against the mattress, stilling the automatic surge of her body, and sought her out with his tongue, laving her much like a cat. Nearly mindless in sensation, she fought against him even while struggling to get closer. He controlled her with almost no effort, occasionally turning his face and softly biting the fleshy part of her inner thigh. Each sharp nip added to her pleasure, taking her a little higher, forcing her a little closer to the edge until she was beyond desperate.

"*Come.*" Alec gave his command with supreme confidence, then caught her small bud between his teeth to torment her with his tongue, and Celia screamed, fully obedient, arching her back, digging her fingers into the mattress, so overwhelmed with emotion and sensation she could do nothing more than ride along on the wave of extreme pleasure. Nothing, no past experience, no mature knowledge, had prepared her for this.

When it ended, she couldn't exactly say. Her body buzzed, her mind felt blurry. One minute she'd been insensible, and the next, Alec was leaving the bed.

She barely got her eyes open. "Alec?" The word was a breathy whisper.

He turned, kissed her hard right on the mouth, making her eyes widen a little, then growled, "I need an icy shower, babe. Just stay put and give me a minute. Then we'll get breakfast and talk."

He stalked, beautifully, sinfully naked into the bathroom and kicked the door shut. A second later the shower started.

Still staring at the closed door, still seeing that sexy, naked, hard-muscled behind, Celia blew out a slow breath. *Oh wow.* She wasn't prepared for this, didn't know how to handle it. Why did he keep giving her pleasure while taking none for himself? Did he expect her to think he didn't want her? Ha. He'd looked ready to self-destruct when he left the bed, all flushed, hot, ready man. Any other man *wouldn't* have left the damn bed.

Did this have something to do with what he'd told her last night? That ridiculous business about insisting she ask for him? Actually, she thought she had. Several times.

She may have even begged.

She'd also thought she knew about sex, but then, no one had ever told her about Alec Sharpe.

6

SHE'D EATEN NEARLY as much as he had. Alec grinned. The little lady had worked up an appetite. Or rather, he'd worked one up for her.

Damn, he could still taste her, and she'd been much tastier than the eggs and ham. Delicious, so sweet she could easily become an addiction. Everything about Celia was unique, so he wasn't at all surprised. His own restraint was the only shocker. How the hell he'd summoned up the willpower to walk away from her was the million dollar question. But he knew. Even now, she wouldn't quite meet his eyes, and she blushed every time he spoke to her.

She was ashamed, embarrassed, and he wanted to drag her back off to bed and keep her there until she got over her absurd hang-ups.

He hadn't realized he'd begun scowling at her until she slapped down her fork and finally looked him square in the eyes. "What are you up to, Alec?"

He choked on a sudden laugh, something he hadn't done in too many years to count. His day-to-day life didn't consist of lighthearted moments. Few people ever used that hostile tone with him, even fewer demanded answers of him. But Celia, though she was pink-cheeked and fidgety, managed to dredge up the spunk. He took a sip of his coffee, letting her stew, then said calmly, "Just waiting for you to accept a few facts."

She actually sneered at him, forcing him to repress another smile. "What facts? That you're a great lover? Ha! I'll never know, will I, when you keep running from the bed."

He would not let her rile him. Her bravado was a front for the real issue—her hurt feelings. And he regretted that. "I'm good enough, but then you make the effort a real pleasure."

She started to stand and he caught her wrist. "Don't cause a scene, honey. Remember, you have a cover around here to protect."

With the meanest look he could have imagined on such a sweet face, she reluctantly resettled herself.

"Now," he said, keeping his hold on her delicate wrist, "I wasn't insulting you. No, just listen. I want you, Celia. Don't doubt that, but like I told you, I'll be damned before I add to your skewed perspective on what's shameful and what isn't."

She toyed with her napkin. "After what you...we did, we might as well have...you know."

Taking another sip of unwanted coffee, he stalled for time. He had to play his hand carefully, had to measure his every word. "Do you feel dirty this morning, honey?"

Judging by her reaction, he should have measured a little more. Her small hands fisted on the table and the color in her face now was from anger, not embarrassment.

"Is that it, Alec?" She spoke in a low whisper, mindful of the one other couple in the café so early in

the morning. "Are you out to use my own weak-
nesses against me? If you're hoping I'll give up on
Hannah and go home just because you can make
me—"

She gasped when he stood and pulled her up from
her chair. "Not another word, lady."

She jerked her arm free and turned to walk out.
Alec threw money on the table and followed her.
Leaving the restaurant was fine by him; what he
planned to say to her would be better said without an
audience.

Celia stomped across the motel parking lot and
started up the outside stairs to her room without once
turning to see if Alec followed. That added to his rage
as he wrapped his arm around her waist and steered
her toward his truck instead. When she started to
fight him, he tightened his grip. "Oh no, you're not
getting off that easy. We have plans to make today
and regardless of your temper, we'll stay on sched-
ule. You want to save little Hannah, well fine. But
we're definitely going to get a few things straightened out first."

The day was already sweltering, and heat rolled off
the blacktop parking lot in waves. It was nothing
compared to his ignited temper. He opened the truck
door then waited while she threw him a malicious
look before climbing in.

Alec slammed his own door hard enough to rattle
the interior. He jammed the key in the ignition, hit the
button to lock both doors, then gripped the steering
wheel with all his might. Losing his control wouldn't
help anything. Oh, Celia was doing her best to act un-

concerned, but he knew her well enough by now to read her every thought, and he had her nervous. Rather than cooling his temper, that put it over the edge and he jerked around to face her, barking, "*God-dammit*, I would never hurt you so stop cowering in the damn corner!"

She bristled up like an angry racoon. Shooting across the seat to face him nose to nose, she yelled, "You don't scare me!"

A red haze clouded his vision. Very slowly, his arms crept around her, keeping her from retreating. "Then tell me what you're thinking, damn it."

She hesitated only a moment, biting her lip before lifting her chin. She didn't try to escape his hold, and that was a blessing, because Alec felt entirely too possessive and territorial to have her inching away. He wanted her close, and he wanted her to admit to liking it, too.

She touched the front of his shirt. "I don't understand you, Alec. I don't know what you're doing or why you suddenly got so mad."

Alec dropped his forehead against hers, and allowed his hands to tighten on her just a bit, bringing her breasts closer, arching her into his body. He took several slow breaths, regaining control. "I'm sorry."

Her eyes widened and her mouth fell open. Obviously she hadn't expected that. And with good reason. He couldn't remember ever apologizing to anyone before, at least, not since he'd been a kid, not since he'd learned his own lessons.

To further surprise them both, he admitted, "I don't like it when you compare me to Raymond."

Celia shook her head, her confusion apparent. "I didn't."

"Oh yeah you did." He released her to face the windshield, staring out at the hazy sunshine and the few clouds in the sky. "You do it all the damn time. Raymond is the one who used you, not me. Raymond is the one who played games with your body and your feelings. Not me."

She bristled again, her face going hot and her eyes glittering, though this reaction was tempered with confusion. "And you don't think what you did last night or this morning qualifies as a game?"

"No." He turned his head toward her, but his hands gripped the steering wheel so tight his knuckles turned white. "When I'm making love to you, it's strictly for pleasure, mine and yours. It's not to hurt you in any way, or to manipulate you."

She barked out an incredulous laugh. "You never take any pleasure!"

He stared at her. "Just seeing you is a pleasure. If you think I can look at you buck naked, that I can make you scream when you come, and not enjoy the hell out of it, you're not as smart as I thought you were."

Her face flamed again, but her eyes turned softer, more accepting. "That's not what I'm talking about, Alec."

He thumped the steering wheel once with a fist. "I want you to trust me. That's all. I want you to see that what's between us is damn good."

She crossed her arms beneath her breasts. "For as long as it lasts?"

He didn't like the way she said that, as something of a challenge. But he wouldn't let her corner him into making false promises. He turned away and started the truck. "Nothing lasts forever. But in the meantime, we're wasting a hell of an opportunity."

"What if I want more, Sharpe?" Her bravado had her once again facing him down, and this time he resented the hell out of it. "What if I want all the things Dane and Angel have?"

He swallowed, feeling a sudden constriction in his chest. He almost said, *What if I don't have that to give,* but he bit the words back at the last moment. Giving away that much of himself wouldn't do.

He put the truck in gear and pulled into the early-morning traffic, giving himself plenty of time to think.

"Alec?"

Now she sounded uncertain again and he hated it. "I don't know. Until Dane found Angel, I'd have said it wasn't possible. But things seem to be...working out for them." He knew he sounded like an idiot, but this was one topic that made him extremely nervous. And he didn't like the feeling worth a damn.

She laughed, incredulous. "They adore each other!"

Turning a corner in the road, he asked, as nonchalantly as possible, "Do you adore me?"

A thick silence filled the truck and he felt himself beginning to sweat despite the icy air blasting from the truck's air conditioner. "That's what I figured. So why all the questions about happily ever after? Why not just take what we can for right now and enjoy it?"

She avoided that question by asking one of her own. "Where are we going?"

"I have to find a place to stay other than with you. It's possible Jacobs will have you watched. If I bunk down with you on occasion, that's fine. He'll expect it of you and it'll only shore up your image of being the type of woman he can approach. But moving in with you entirely is out of the question. Jacobs doesn't prey on women who have protectors."

"You're finally admitting that I was right? That Jacobs is scum using women like Hannah? My, my. This is turning into one eventful day."

Alec hid his grin behind a look of reproach. She was so full of herself, taunting him. But he preferred that any day over her insecurities or her damn questions about the future. "I did my research, honey. I know what Jacobs is capable of and I never denied that he's a bastard, only whether or not Hannah appreciated the setup he gave her. If she's really unhappy with him, why doesn't she just call her mother and go home?"

Another of those heavy, uncomfortable silences filled the truck and Alec regretted his words. He didn't want to put her back in a dark mood. But then she turned to face him, and her determination was plain to see.

"You wouldn't know what it's like, Alec. You're strong and independent and able to take care of yourself and any situation. I can't imagine anyone or anything ever really hurting you."

She made it sound like an insult, as if along with his strengths he'd become too empty to care. "I'm not invincible, damn it." Far from it, he thought, briefly focusing on the past and a time that was too painful to remember for long.

"You sure seem invincible to me. You see everything as black and white and you always stick to your convictions. But I remember how ashamed I was after Raymond turned out to be such a user."

"Celia..." He didn't want to talk about Raymond again. If he could, he gladly would have erased the man from both their memories.

She didn't plan to give him any choice. "You can just sit there and listen, Alec Sharpe!" When he remained silent, she continued, though she was obviously ruffled just a bit. "I started wondering about Raymond long before I knew how truly evil he was. But by then, everyone knew I had planned to marry him, and my mother accepted him, and you and Dane never once questioned me about him."

Alec glared at her. "Dane thought you were happy. He didn't want to do anything that would hurt you."

"And what was your excuse?"

Alec narrowed his eyes again and said through his teeth, "I knew if I got too damn close to you, which included poking my nose into your business, I wouldn't be able to keep my hands off you. I wanted to get rid of Raymond just so he wouldn't be in my way."

Celia blinked at him, awed by this outpouring of confessions. "I...I had no idea."

"Bull. From the second we met, you felt the pull as much as I did. Don't lie about it now."

She tightened her mouth, but didn't deny it. "All

right, maybe I had a clue or two. But you're not an easy man to figure out and I had my hands full already. I was too embarrassed to admit what an awful mistake I'd made with Raymond, that I didn't love him and didn't want to marry him, that I had been duped so thoroughly."

"You weren't the only one he had fooled."

"He didn't fool you. Right from the start you seemed to despise him, and Raymond never understood it. He'd talk about you sometimes, in this almost fearful, reverent way. But he got really angry if I even mentioned your name."

"You mentioned me to him?"

"Oh, for pity's sake. Don't look so smug." Celia rolled her eyes and shook her head. "Mostly I talked about what a reprehensible character you seemed to be."

Alec laughed.

Another silence stretched out, and Alec glanced at her.

Celia wrung her hands. Speaking in a soft, nearly audible voice, she said, "Whenever I mentioned putting the wedding off, Raymond would..."

"Celia." He wasn't at all sure he needed to hear this.

"He'd take me to bed."

She closed her eyes and Alec wished he could do the same. Thinking of her with Raymond tortured him. But this was obviously something she wanted to get off her chest, and if it would ease her, he'd listen. "Go on."

"Everything he'd taught me was so new and exciting. At first I thought I loved him, and that made it seem okay. But little by little, I resented the way he used my...sexuality against me. He'd taunt me over how easy I was and tell me how shocked my family would be if we didn't marry considering I acted like a...a..." She hesitated, drawing a deep breath.

Alec reached over and clasped both her hands. "Like a what, honey?"

"A bitch in heat."

He squeezed her fingers and offered her a slight smile. "Then what would that make me, since I can't seem to think about anything other than staking a claim on you? Right now, Celia, if you asked me and meant it, I'd pull this truck over and you'd find your jeans around your ankles before you had time to blink."

She stared at him, shocked, then she laughed. "Why, you sweet talker you."

Alec laughed, too, though he wanted and needed her so bad he didn't know how much longer he could hold out. "I have no finesse where you're concerned, honey. You make me feel raw."

She drew a long slow breath and stared at him. "You really are a sweet talker."

Alec shrugged that off. "I keep telling you, Raymond was an ass. Any man who had you and didn't appreciate it is too stupid to waste breath on."

As he finished that declaration, he pulled into a motel and parked his truck. Turning in his seat, he drew her closer and kissed her, moving so his mouth opened, his tongue immediately stroking deep. Against her lips, he whispered, "After I've had you,

you won't have the energy to think of him. That's a promise. The only question now is when."

THE MOTEL ALEC CHOSE based on immediate vacancy was actually fairly close to her own by the way the crow flies. However, using the busy roads, it took a good twenty minutes to reach her. This concerned Alec, but Celia insisted there wasn't anything she'd need him for that couldn't wait that long. She didn't want to add to Alec's pressure, since he was actually working with her under duress.

His motel was even seedier than her own, with a horrid bathroom complete with cracked tiles and she'd be willing to bet a lack of hot water. But Alec never blinked an eye at the utilitarian setting. He stowed his few things, made a couple of quick calls, then bundled Celia back into his truck. They spent most of the morning and afternoon shopping.

By the time they were done, Alec had purchased a cell phone for her and a few other precautionary items, like pepper spray and a "screamer," a small can that literally screamed when the nozzle was compressed. Celia tried it once, and got to see just how fast Alec could move. He had it out of her hand and was glaring at her within a heartbeat. She'd felt compelled to offer a mumbled apology, but in truth, she had to hide her smile.

Alec really didn't frighten her anymore. In fact, he almost made her feel cherished.

The precautions he took with her safety didn't feel like a lack of trust, but rather very deep concern for a woman he cared about.

She was pondering that vague possibility when Alec said, "Tell me again what my number is."

"Alec, I have it memorized. We've been over it a dozen times."

"Tell me anyway. I want to make damn sure that if something goes wrong, you know it by heart. You might not have time to think about it..."

She recited the number.

"Good. Now, I put the number in the memory, so all you have to do is dial 1, but—"

"Alec." She shook her head at him. "If the number is in the memory, why did I have to learn it?"

He touched her cheek. "What if Jacobs catches on to you and takes your phone? Or what if you manage to lose it? You might have to use a pay phone. It's best to cover all the bases, babe."

"Okay." She no longer felt the need to fight him on every issue. Strange how sometime during their drive, her attitude had changed. Oh, she was still wary. And she didn't yet trust herself to give in to him completely. But she also wanted him, and she knew he felt the same. Only he suffered no guilt, no embarrassment at all. He'd told her that her sex drive was "healthy."

Around him, she was in the peak of health.

"Yoo-hoo. Miss Carter?" Alec waved a hand in front of her face. "You want to join me here so we can make these plans, or do you want to stand there day-dreaming?"

"You have my undivided attention, Alec."

The look he gave her was skeptical. "Uh-huh. I could tell you were on full alert." He leaned against the wall of her motel room and crossed his arms over his chest. "Do you have something sexy to wear tonight?"

"Yes, I do."

"Make sure it's not too sexy, all right? I don't want to be forced to diffuse a riot."

She felt her cheeks warm. Alec honestly thought she was sexy enough to turn heads, and his confidence helped shore up her own. "I'll be discreetly sexy."

Another skeptical look, as if he didn't think such a thing was possible. "Show up on time. I'll be there around four o'clock, but you shouldn't show up until seven. I don't want anyone to think we're together in any way."

"What should I say if someone asks me? After all, they all noticed us leaving together yesterday."

Alec shrugged. "Say I was lousy in bed."

Celia choked and had to turn quickly away. She paced the small confines of the room, stepping around her exercise equipment. "Maybe I'll say you bored me."

"Whatever. But remember to pay me no mind, no matter what I do."

That had her whipping around. "What do you plan to do?"

"Flirt. Pick up other women."

Groping for the edge of the bed, Celia sat down. Alec came over to stand directly in front of her, which put her eye level with his zipper. He crossed his arms over his chest and growled, "You already know I don't want anyone but you, Celia. But I have to act like the average bar groupie, and that means I'll have to act drunk, obnoxious, and horny."

Celia gulped. "Will you actually—"

"Sleep with anyone? Hell no. My health means a little more to me than that."

She wanted to crumble in relief, but instead she pushed to her feet and tried to get Alec to back up. He didn't.

"I need to start getting ready, so you should go. I have to shower and do my hair and—"

Alec cupped her face. "I hate this. I hate letting you walk into that place and I hate knowing what all those creeps will be thinking about you." He kissed her, gently, teasingly. "Promise me you'll be extra careful. And don't go anywhere with anyone, no matter what. If Jacobs really does know where Hannah is, we'll find her. But I don't want anything to happen to you in the process."

Tenderness threatened to break her control. She forced a smile and voluntarily kissed him this time, just as teasing as he had been. "I promise to be careful if you do. Don't let some hussy have her way with you."

His gaze turned hot and he stepped away from her. "These days I'm saving myself for you. And if you make me wait much longer, I swear I'm going to explode. Keep that in mind, will you?"

Then he walked out the door, checking it to make certain it had locked. Celia sank back down on the mattress. Keep it in mind? It was damn near all she could think about.

7

THE MUSIC WAS LOUD when Celia entered the bar. Smoke hung heavy in the air and she felt the eyes of a dozen men watching her as she made her way to a bar stool.

Then she spotted Alec.

In the middle of the dance floor, moving much too slowly for the fast beat of the music, he held a woman with long pale hair and pretended to dance. One of his large hands was curved on her behind and Celia, taken aback by the scene though he'd warned her, froze to the spot.

She wanted to kill him.

Her heart seemed to leap around in her chest, her vision blurred. Then Alec looked up at her, grinned and winked, before releasing the woman and walking her way. He stopped in front of her, his expression arrogant, his black eyes dilated. He flicked the end of her nose in an insolent manner and bent to her ear.

"It's a game, Celia, and you're about to blow it." He kissed her cheek and walked away.

Slouching in a booth at the back of the bar, he called for another drink, and the waitress he'd just been making love to hurried to fetch it.

Belatedly remembering herself, Celia flipped her

hair behind her ear and gave him a "hmmpf" shrug, then sat down and ordered her own beverage. Her mind was in such a turmoil, filled with images of Alec with that *other* woman, she barely heard the bartender when he leaned close and asked her if she was all right.

"Oh, don't be silly." She gave him her most dazzling smile while fluttering a hand in dismissal. "I'm perfectly fine."

The bartender eyed her pensively while polishing a glass. "You ask me, you looked a little poleaxed to see your beau here."

Feigning shock, she said, "My beau?" Then with another twittering laugh: "You mean that ragtag bum? Well, I was surprised to see him here considering I'd hoped not to—ever again." She giggled. "Sometimes loneliness can make us do the dumbest things, and going out with that one marks the top of the list."

"Didn't work out quite as you planned, huh?"

The bartender now grinned, too, and Celia leaned closer still, pretending to share a confidence. She whispered, "He's not real bright, and he's entirely too...well...*rough.*"

"He does look like a mean hombre, at that. He didn't hurt you, did he?"

"No, of course not. I didn't mean that. It's just that I couldn't get rid of him. He wanted to move in on me! I had to be almost cruel to get rid of him. I felt a little bad about it, but I can barely afford to take care of myself right now, much less someone else."

The bartender patted her hand. "You did the right thing."

Suddenly a new voice intruded and Celia felt every hair on her body tingle. "If you have any more problems with him, you can let me know."

Slowly she turned, and sure enough, Mr. Jacobs had taken the seat beside her. The bartender was quick with the introductions, beaming all the while.

"Miss, this is Marc Jacobs. He owns this bar, among other things, and tends to take the safety of the female clientele real personal."

"That I do, Wally. Especially when the lady is so lovely." His pale blue eyes glittered at Celia, and her blush wasn't in the least feigned. The man was sizing her up, and she'd never felt so exposed, or so disgraced, in her life. She swallowed hard and thought of Alec, sitting only a short distance away.

Looking at Jacobs through her lashes, she whispered in acknowledgment, "Mr. Jacobs."

"Marc. I insist. And you are?" He slowly took her hand from her lap and squeezed her fingers in a familiar way. Repulsed, Celia wanted to jerk back, but more than that, she wanted to find Hannah. And somehow she knew Alec was watching, that he was aware of every little movement she or Jacobs made. She wanted to prove to him that she could do this, and his nearness gave her courage and determination.

"All right, Marc." Her smile was complimenting, teasing. "I'm Celia. Celia..." She hesitated. She didn't want to give him her actual last name in case he had her investigated. But the only other last name that came to mind was Alec's. Wincing inside at her own audacity, she said, "Celia Sharpe."

"Celia. It's a lovely name. Would you like to join me at my table?"

Flirting, she said, "I'd dearly love to join you at your table. Thank you."

He held her hand as she slid off the stool. Her dress, a cream-colored, silky summer shift cut low in front and back, and held up by tiny cap sleeves, smoothed over her legs as she walked. It fell narrow and straight to just below her knees and was accented by the dreaded, uncomfortable push-up bra, minimal jewelry, and strappy sandals. She caught Jacobs staring at her breasts as they made their way across the crowded floor. When she went to sit, Jacobs's hand strayed over her waist and her hip.

Celia's stomach roiled.

Seconds later a waitress delivered her drink and a fresh one for Jacobs.

"So," he said, smiling at her with impeccable, perfect white teeth, "you're new around here, aren't you? What are you in town for?"

Trying for a look of coy bashfulness, Celia bit her lip and stared down at her hands. "Well, I suppose I wanted excitement most of all. I got really tired of hanging around my small hometown. I used to live close to my grandmother, but she passed away, and then there was really no reason for me to stay there."

Looking falsely sympathetic, Jacobs asked, "No other relatives?"

She shook her head, then sipped at her drink. "No.

I'm on my own, and that's sort of a good thing, don't you think? No responsibilities, I mean."

"You could look at it that way." He touched the back of her hand with one finger, a gesture meant to be sympathetic, but felt totally smarmy to Celia considering the look in his eyes. "No husband, or at least a fiancé? I would think a woman as beautiful as you would have been captured by now by some lucky man."

Again she bit her lip. She could just imagine what his idea of *capture* entailed. "I had a few boyfriends. But they were all yokels. They had these plans of settling down and starting a family." She was every day of twenty-six years old, but for as long as she could remember, folks had told her she looked younger. She hoped it was true, or she was about to make an awful fool of herself.

She cleared her throat and said, "I'm too young to do all that. I have tons of time to settle down after I've done all the things I'd like to do."

Jacobs studied her, making her squirm, then he asked, "You're definitely too young. About twenty or so, right?"

She beamed at him, affecting her ditzy look. "Twenty-one, free and fully legal. Marriage should be when you're, like, thirty or something, right?"

His smile was indulgent. "Absolutely. So Celia, tell me about these things you'd like to do with your life."

She blushed again. A pale complexion had always been the bane of her life, but now she counted herself lucky. She flipped her hair over her shoulders, shrugged and whispered, "You'll think I'm silly."

His fingers drifted over her cheek. "Not at all."

She drew a deep breath, more to steady her stomach than to draw forth her nerve. "Well, my grandmother used to say I was pretty enough to be a model." She peeked up at him. "I know I'm not, but it's something I've always dreamed about. Seeing myself in a magazine. Or maybe being in commercials." She shivered. "It would be so wonderful!"

Jacobs toyed with his glass, swirling the amber liquid around as if in deep thought, while staring at her. His stare was nothing like Alec's. It unnerved her, that much was familiar, but with Alec she felt charged and alive, with this man she felt dread and bone-deep discomfort, something very close to fear.

She sighed. "I know. Fanciful dreams. But I figured I had to at least try or I'd never be able to forgive myself. Only I didn't get much farther than this before I started to run out of money and I have no idea who to contact, or how to go about getting the attention of an agent. Tomorrow I'm going to be practical though. I'm going to find a job somewhere, save up more money, then get started again."

"Where will you work?" he asked with concern.

Shrugging, Celia said, "At a restaurant I suppose. I've seen plenty of signs up for waitresses and they say the tips are good."

"Oh, I've no doubt you'll make plenty in tips, but a job like that would be an insult to a woman as lovely as you." He dragged one long finger around the rim of his glass, as if coming to a decision, then he nodded. "Would you be shocked, Celia, if I told you I was an agent?"

She opened her eyes as wide as she could get them. "You're kidding, right?"

"No." He smiled again. "Celia, would you pose for me?"

She almost swallowed her tongue. Her pulse raced, her heart jumped. "I beg your pardon?"

His look was calculating and predatory. "Along with owning this bar, I have many connections in the fashion world. I'm actually a fairly well-known agent and I work with lots of girls. I want to see if you're comfortable showing yourself to advantage. If you are, why then, I think I may have a proposition for you."

Since she had absolutely no intention of going anywhere alone with this man, she immediately stood and held out her arms. Smiling with false hope, she turned a pirouette and struck several provocative poses. Looking eager, she asked, "Should I stand on a table? I would you know. I desperately want a chance to prove myself."

Jacobs laughed in genuine delight. "That won't be necessary. And besides, I think your boyfriend might object to that. He looks ready to self-destruct."

She resisted the nearly impossible urge to look at Alec. "My boyfriend?"

Jacobs nodded to the other side of the bar. "You caught his attention with your little show and somehow I get the impression he'd like another go at you."

Celia glanced in the direction Jacobs indicated, taking her time before finally focusing on Alec. She saw that damn waitress now perched in his lap, one of her hands under Alec's shirt, stroking his belly. Alec seemed to be giving her mouth-to-mouth.

Celia's disgust was very real. "He's a macho pig. Believe me, he's of no concern at all."

"Excellent. I just thought it prudent to ask."

Celia eagerly reseated herself. "So what is your proposition?"

Again, Jacobs laughed at her enthusiasm. "There's a party tonight. A lot of important people will be there. I'd like you to come."

Her heart nearly exploded at this incredible chance to make headway. Surely Hannah would be there, and if Celia could only talk to her alone for a moment, she might be able to get the girl to go home.

Interrupting her thoughts, Jacobs reached out for her hand again. "We can leave here in an hour or so. I'll take you myself."

She remembered her precarious position and ducked her face, moaning. "Gosh, I wish I could! This is just awful."

His fingers tightened almost cruelly on her own. "What is it?"

Working up a tear, she said, "I can't go looking like this!" She splayed her hands over her bosom, indicating her attire. "My dress is totally inappropriate. I want to make a grand impression when I do meet someone, not have them thinking I'm a country bumpkin."

He stared at her hands, or rather, her breasts beneath them. He licked his lips. "You're right, of course. But it's not a problem. We'll stop by your room and you can change into something a little...dressier."

Not in this lifetime. Shaking her head, she conjured up the most dejected look she could manage. "You don't understand. I *am* a bumpkin. I don't own anything fancy enough for an important party."

Jacobs checked his watch, letting a little irritation show through. "The boutique owner on Fifth and Main is a friend of mine. I'll call her and tell her you're coming."

Celia was stunned. "But I can't afford..."

Stalling her objection in midsentence, he withdrew his wallet and pulled out a wad of bills. Celia stared wide-eyed, beyond being shocked. Thumbing out a string of twenties, he rolled them and stuffed them into her hand. "Buy yourself something spectacular and sexy—Shirley will help you decide. Leave everything in her capable hands. She works with me often. And then take a cab to the party. Arriving a few minutes late will help you make an entrance. It'll intrigue certain fellows even more."

She stared at the money in her hand. "Are you serious?"

Scribbling an address onto a napkin, Jacobs chuckled. "Absolutely. Believe me, honey, I can afford a new outfit for you, and when you get your first photo shoot, you can pay me back with interest. Agreed?"

"You...you really think there's a possibility?"

"I think it's a done deal." He handed her the napkin. "Just tell the cabbie to deliver you to this address. The doorman will pay him. Be there by ten o'clock, and in the meantime I'll talk you up. You'll make a huge splash tonight."

She felt staggered by how quickly things had progressed, and how incredibly easy it seemed. "This is like a dream." *More like a nightmare. Was this how Hannah had gotten sucked in, so fast she didn't have time to think?*

"Celia?" He tipped up her chin and his eyes were direct, a vague warning shining through the pale blue. "Don't disappoint me now."

A fine trembling had invaded her body. Slowly she stood, moving away from his touch. "I'll be there. And thank you. Thank you so much."

"It's my pleasure."

As she walked away, she thought of how she could warn Alec, how she could let him know what had transpired. But he wasn't even looking at her. He was slumped in the booth, head back, eyes closed, the waitress still on his lap, chewing on his damn neck. Celia hoped she hit an artery. When she saw Alec's hand go to the woman's rump again, she set her teeth and marched on outside, quickly summoning a cab.

It didn't matter that Alec claimed it was a game. She needed him now, and he was playing with another woman. The jealousy was something she'd never experienced before, a devouring evil inside her, making her breath come fast and her heart thump too hard. It staggered her, overriding the euphoria of all she'd accomplished tonight, the headway she'd made.

Rather than planning on how to handle the rest of the evening, she wanted to wreak havoc, to beat on

Alec and make him promise her he'd... The thought struck her like a smack to the head, nearly knocking her off her high heels. Dear God.

She was in love with Alec Sharpe.

Slumping back in the cab seat, she groaned and covered her face with her hands. Of all the incredible things to happen. And she had the awful suspicion she'd actually fallen for the tough guy some time ago—like when she'd very first met him. The sight of him excited her. The smell of him excited her. The way he talked and walked and his roughness mixed with his protective instincts...

Well hell. It didn't get much worse than this.

ALEC SAT IN THE DARK, just waiting. Every muscle in his body felt tight, almost quivering, and he thought he might explode at any moment if...

The lock on the door clicked and slowly opened. He didn't move except for the narrowing of his eyes. Every nerve was on alert, ready, almost anxious for any confrontation that would allow him to let off a little steam. And then he recognized her scent; he knew Celia, body and soul, on an elemental level that gripped him gut-deep. He could have picked her out of a hundred women just by the touch of her skin or her arousing fragrance, not store-bought but a part of the woman. *His woman.*

The fact that it was Celia entering, rather than an intruder, was almost better. It certainly allowed some of his panic to recede, making the way clear for his rage. He waited for the door to close so no one would hear the argument about to erupt. When she flipped on a light switch and turned to see him, she gasped, then immediately went on the defensive.

Clutching the front of her dress over her heart with a fist, she said, "Alec! You scared me half to death! What are you doing sneaking in here?"

He came slowly, angrily to his feet. Gaze pinning her, he stalked forward. There was very little talking he planned to do until a few of his questions were answered. "Where the hell have you been?"

He didn't recognize his own voice, but he'd been through twenty kinds of hell in the past hour and he didn't like feeling that much, not when he'd spent a good part of life freezing out deeper emotions and feelings. Yet she consistently, repeatedly, *deliberately* made him feel things.

He didn't touch her, merely loomed over her, feeling every bit as much a demon as he'd often been accused of being.

She glared at him. "If you hadn't been playing sucky-face with that scrawny waitress, I'd have been able to get your attention when I left."

"I saw you leave, damn it." His teeth ached from clenching them so tightly; did she honestly think he hadn't seen every little move she'd made?

He reached out and slowly crowded her back against the wall. She didn't look intimidated, she just looked mad. Good, misery loved company. "Why the hell didn't you wait outside for me?"

"Because I couldn't." Her little nose went into the air. "I had to buy a dress for a party tonight."

A red haze covered his vision. "Forget it."

She suddenly gasped. "You're drunk!"

"Not even close." Her breasts brushed his chest and his stomach tightened.

"I can smell the alcohol on your breath, Alec."

"One glass of whiskey. And believe me, it'd take more than that, so stop trying to turn the tide. You've got some explaining to do, lady, and I'm about clean out of patience."

She searched his face, then suddenly punched his chest. "You have lipstick on your *ear*, damn it! And you smell like a French whore."

What that had to do with anything he couldn't imagine. "She was all over me, Celia. Until I can change clothes, we'll both have to put up with it."

"Wrong. I don't have to put up with anything." She glanced at the clock beside the bed and muttered, "I've only got a half an hour to get changed and get to the party. Hopefully it's not too far away."

Propping both hands beside her head, imprisoning her with his body, he fought to maintain his control. "You're not going to any damn party, baby."

"Oh yes I am! This is the best opportunity in the world to find Hannah. I have to go."

"No."

She drew herself up. "I don't have time for this, Alec." Then just as quickly she asked with a sneer, "Did you enjoy yourself at the bar?"

He wrapped one large hand around her skull to hold her still, then leaned forward until their noses touched. "With Jacobs leering at you?" The rage bubbled up again and he squeezed his eyes shut. "You don't have any idea how damn hard that was for me, do you?"

"You looked plenty distracted to me."

"Which was the point, damn it!"

She blinked at his raised tone. "You really didn't enjoy kissing her?"

Shoving himself away from the wall with a burst of energy, he paced, then immediately stalked back. He grabbed her hand and pressed it to his fly. "That's reserved for you, lady." She started to pull away but he wouldn't let her. A small groan escaped him. "A sheik's harem wouldn't do it for me now, not when I'm wanting you."

Her fingers curled, caressing him. In a whisper, she asked, "Do you mean that, Alec?"

Staring at her hard, he said, "I've told you all along it's you. If I only wanted to get laid, I damn sure could have done that long before tonight, and with a hell of a lot less trouble than you give me."

Her breath came a little faster and she nervously licked her lips.

Alec groaned, all his anger transferring into redhot need. He wanted to brand her, put his mark on her for all the world to see. He wanted her acceptance and understanding.

To block the assault of emotions he didn't want to deal with, he kissed her, long and hard and with so much possession and passion she all but forgot about the damn party.

But of course, she couldn't.

In trembling tones, she said, "I want you, too, Alec, I really do."

He leaned back to look at her, his own body shaking.

"But I have to do this. Please." Her eyes pleaded with him and he turned away, but she caught him by the waistband of his jeans and held on. It was either give in to her, or drag her in his wake. "Alec, *please?*"

He had to think, but there really wasn't time. She'd said she had only a half hour. Still without looking at her, not willing to test his control that far, he said, "Tell me everything. Hurry."

She did, and Alec had to agree that the possibilities were endless. Getting into the mind-set of the chase helped to clear his head of the lust. But not completely.

"He even sent me to this shady little boutique where a woman named Shirley dressed me like a damned Thanksgiving turkey, from my earrings down to the sandals I'll wear. I had the feeling this was some sort of arrangement they had, that a lot of girls are paraded through that boutique and outfitted *appropriately.*" In a lower voice, she confided, "Shirley looks like an Alcatraz escapee. Really gave me the willies."

He chewed the side of his mouth, thinking it all through logically before finally accepting that he had little choice in letting her go.

"All right." He turned to glare at her, wanting no misunderstandings. "My instincts as a man tell me to say no way, to tie you to the damn bed and keep you there if necessary. But," he added when she started to object, "as an agent, I know this could be our only opening."

She looked as though she had mixed feelings about his capitulation. "So you agree?"

"Yeah. But I'm going, too. No, don't panic. I'll be outside, but close. If you need me, just hit the button on your phone. Any call at all and I'm coming in, babe, so be careful."

She threw her arms around his neck and squeezed him tight. "I hate to admit it, but I'm glad to know you'll be there."

Holding her so close was like a tonic, both soothing him and setting his blood to pumping. He pressed his nose to her neck and breathed deeply. "Having second thoughts?" She was on tiptoe and he slipped his hands beneath her skirt to fill his palms with her soft bottom. He needed something to tide him over, and touching her was a small consolation.

She groaned, but shook her head. "No, I'm doing this, Alec, I have to. But I feel better about the whole thing, knowing I won't be alone."

Two seconds more of her willing acceptance and he'd crumble. That would sure as hell shoot the night, at the same time demolishing the progress he'd made. Knowing that helped him do the right thing. He pried her arms loose and gently sent her into the bathroom with a firm swat on her perfect fanny. He had a bad feeling about all this, not a gut instinct, which he wouldn't have dared ignore, but just an unsettled feeling in his chest, like a hard fist squeezed around his heart. He didn't like it. "Go get dressed, Celia, before I change my mind. To keep any onlookers from getting suspicious, I'm going out to wait in my car. After the cab picks you up, I'll follow along, but you won't see me, okay?"

"What if Jacobs has guards?"

"They'll never know I'm there."

"You're that good?"

He smiled and deliberately dropped his voice to a low, seductive tone. "I promise to be the best you ever had." He left before she could get her mouth closed or find a suitable comeback. Hopefully he'd have a chance to prove that taunt, and soon.

Most of the world considered him a mean son of a bitch, dangerously lethal, invulnerable, hard-edged. But Celia had never backed down from him. At first her spunk and cursed doggedness, along with her sweet good looks, had merely intrigued him. But now she'd managed to crawl under his skin and he had a feeling her unsettling effect wasn't going to go away any time soon. For awhile there, he'd thought making love to her would help, would wash her out of his system so he could start thinking rationally again, with his brains rather than his libido.

Now, he wasn't so sure.

He hoped she came to reason soon, because he really didn't think he could take much more.

8

HER FACE HURT from smiling, her brain hurt from concentrating so hard on appearing insipid, and every muscle in her body ached from the need to hide herself away. In a house this size, it should have been easy. But not once since she'd entered had she been given a private moment. She felt like a piece of raw meat displayed in the market window.

The brownstone structure was heavily guarded, surrounded by a tall, black, wrought-iron fence complete with automatic locking driveway gate and intercoms at every entrance. Guards stood at several windows, both inside and out. Even if she'd wanted to leave, it would have been impossible.

The outfit Shirley had insisted was perfect hadn't seemed nearly so skimpy in the shop when she'd hurriedly accepted it, as it did now with a largely male audience ogling her every move. The black pantsuit had a loose, low-cut crop top that exposed her cleavage and barely hung low enough to conceal the bottom curves of her breasts. It was briefer than many bathing suit bras she'd seen, and since it hung free from her shoulders, she had to be very careful about how she moved.

Paired with the low-riding, hip-hugger pants, it left a lot of midriff bare. The material was raw silk and

GET A FREE TEDDY BEAR...

You'll love this plush, cuddly Teddy Bear, an adorable accessory for your dressing table, bookcase or desk. Measuring 5 ½" tall, he's soft and brown and has a bright red ribbon around his neck – he's completely captivating! And he's yours *absolutely free*, when you accept this no-risk offer!

▼ CLAIM YOUR FREE BOOKS AND FREE GIFT! RETURN THIS CARD TODAY! ▼

AND TWO FREE BOOKS!

Here's a chance to get **two free Harlequin Temptation®** novels from the Harlequin Reader Service® **absolutely free!**

There's no catch. You're under no obligation to buy anything. We charge nothing – ZERO – for your first shipment. And you don't have to make any minimum number of purchases – not even one!

Find out for yourself why thousands of readers enjoy receiving books by mail from the Harlequin Reader Service®. They like the **convenience of home delivery**...they like getting the best new novels months before they're available in bookstores...and they love our **discount prices!**

Try us and see! Return this card promptly. We'll send your free books and a free Teddy Bear, under the terms explained on the back. We hope you'll want to remain with the reader service – but the choice is always yours!

342 HDL CTKD

142 HDL CTJZ
(H-T-10/99)

Name:
(PLEASE PRINT)

Address: _____ Apt.#: _____

City: _____ State/Prov.: _____ Postal Zip/Code: _____

Offer limited to one per household and not valid to current Harlequin Temptation® subscribers. All orders subject to approval. © 1998 HARLEQUIN ENTERPRISES LTD. ® and ™ are trademarks owned by Harlequin Enterprises Ltd.

PRINTED IN U.S.A.

NO OBLIGATION TO BUY!

The Harlequin Reader Service® — Here's how it works:

Accepting your 2 free books and gift places you under no obligation to buy anything. You may keep the books and gift and return the shipping statement marked "cancel." If you do not cancel, about a month later we'll send you 4 additional novels and bill you just $3.12 each in the U.S., or $3.57 each in Canada, plus 25¢ delivery per book and applicable taxes if any.* That's the complete price and — compared to the cover price of $3.75 in the U.S. and $4.25 in Canada — it's quite a bargain! You may cancel at any time, but if you choose to continue, every month we'll send you 4 more books, which you may either purchase at the discount price or return to us and cancel your subscription.

*Terms and prices subject to change without notice. Sales tax applicable in N.Y. Canadian residents will be charged applicable provincial taxes and GST.

If offer card is missing write to: Harlequin Reader Service, 3010 Walden Ave., P.O. Box 1867, Buffalo, NY 14240-1867

BUSINESS REPLY MAIL
FIRST-CLASS MAIL   PERMIT NO. 717   BUFFALO, NY

POSTAGE WILL BE PAID BY ADDRESSEE

HARLEQUIN READER SERVICE
3010 WALDEN AVE
PO BOX 1867
BUFFALO NY 14240-9952

NO POSTAGE
NECESSARY
IF MAILED
IN THE
UNITED STATES

the slightly flared pants made her legs look longer, especially with the impossibly high-heeled sandals that made merely walking a concerted effort. Dangling gold earring hoops nearly touched her shoulders, and matched the gold chain around her waist, hanging over her exposed navel.

When the men at the party spoke to her, they tended to stare at her belly, or her cleavage. Two of them had the audacity to take her hand and force her into a circle so they could gape at her behind. Several had felt free to stroke her stomach with the backs of their knuckles—and Celia, who thought she'd known all about shame—had nearly closed in on herself. The possessive touches made her stomach turn, and she'd gulped down a few too many drinks trying to shore up her courage.

One thought kept going through her mind: Alec never made her feel like this. His touch excited her and made her tingle and she knew without a doubt he could easily make her beg for his body. But he never would, because what he offered he offered freely and without restriction, respecting her and her desires as natural and healthy.

There was nothing natural or healthy about the way these men looked at her.

"Are you enjoying yourself, Celia?"

She did her best to look awed. "Oh yes, Marc. Everyone is so fascinating. See that man over there? He told me he's a film producer and said he'd like to see me again! Isn't that exciting?"

Marc Jacobs smiled benignly. "Wonderful. I knew

you'd do well. But I have even better news. A fellow colleague would like to talk to you privately."

Her heart seemed to shudder and die in midbeat. She stared at him stupidly.

"Oh, now don't get nervous. You'll do fine." He replaced her empty wineglass with a full one from the tray of a passing waitress. Celia automatically sipped. "You look unquestionably edible, Celia, so I'm not at all surprised that Blair noticed you. He freelances for several major magazines, and if I don't miss my guess, he's already picturing you in several spreads. As your acting agent, I recommend you do your best to ingratiate yourself with him."

Celia was busy trying to cover her nervousness, hoping to come up with a way to avoid yet another isolated meeting, when she and Jacobs were approached by two young women. They were each beautiful, putting Celia to disgrace. One had caramel-colored skin and wide, slanted cat eyes and a generous mouth. Her hair was ruthlessly short, but the style suited her high cheekbones and bold features.

The other woman had long, sleek, flowing black hair. Her skin was flawless, very pale, and she had green eyes fringed by lush lashes that added startling color to her face. She was tall, topping Celia by several inches, and her body was willowy, bordering on waiflike. Both women were grinning, sipping drinks, and appeared happy.

Jacobs put one arm around each and made introductions. "Celia, I asked Jade and Hannah to show you around. They're familiar with everyone here and can help you get acclimated."

Celia nearly bit her tongue. *Hannah.* And the girl was impeccably dressed in designer clothing, her face radiant, her expression carefree. Had Alec been right? Was she wasting her time?

With a bold squeeze to each woman's derriere, Jacobs excused himself. He told Celia he'd be back shortly to escort her in to the private meeting.

As soon as he was gone, Jade rubbed her bottom. "Damn, I hate when he does that." She grinned at Celia and stuck out her hand. "So you're new? I hope you're not one of those wide-eyed hopefuls, though truth to tell, you look a lot older than most of the girls Marc brings around."

Jade looked about fifteen but was surely older. She shook Celia's hand, then turned pleading eyes on Hannah. "Can you do the show and tell? I want to get off my feet for awhile. My legs are killing me, and with Marc gone, this might be my only chance to rest."

Hannah's smile was genuine. "Sure thing." She looped arms with Celia. "We'll tour around and get acquainted. But find someplace private to crash. If Marc finds you hiding, you know he won't like it."

With a crooked smile that made her look even younger, Jade said, "I was thinking of a broom closet, actually." Flicking them an airy wave, she walked away, leaving Hannah chuckling behind her.

Celia tried to take advantage of her private time with the girl. "I'm Celia Sharpe," she improvised.

Hannah smiled again. "I'm just Hannah, you know, like Cher." She took Celia's glass and put it on a table already littered with an overflowing ashtray and a few crumpled napkins. "You've had enough of that, haven't you? You look a bit tipsy."

"I don't drink much," Celia admitted. "But here, someone is constantly—"

"Giving you a new one, I know. I think the men like to keep us tipsy. You can imagine why."

Celia stared at her, hoping to gain her confidence. "Why?"

But Hannah just laughed and shook her head. Celia would have liked to have Hannah's last name verified, but the girl matched the description she'd gotten from Mrs. Barrington, so that was good enough for her.

"What are we supposed to be doing, Hannah?"

"Well, for now, just mingling. If you see anyone looking at you, smile, flirt, encourage him with a look, that sort of thing."

Carefully, Celia asked, "And that'll help us get modeling jobs?"

Hannah groaned. "You *are* a hopeful, aren't you? Honey, get realistic. Do you really expect to make it big through this crowd?"

Feeling like a child needing instruction, especially with Hannah's worldly air, Celia said, "Marc told me—"

"Whatever he had to to get you here. Marc appreciates a beautiful woman. And he'll take care of you, so don't worry about that. He'll dress you nice and set you up in a place to live."

"How, if we're not working?"

Hannah gave her a pitying shake of her head. "You know what?" She took Celia's arm and dragged her around a corner of the main room, behind a large planter. "I shouldn't do this, and if you squeal on me—well, let's just say you really shouldn't, okay? But Celia, if you had any sense at all, you'd get out of here right now."

Celia had to look up to meet the girl's eyes. Measuring her words, she said, "I can't. Marc has a meeting set up for me with someone named Blair."

Hannah's face paled and she closed her eyes. "Well. He's not wasting any time with you, is he? It must be because you are a bit older, and he figures you can handle it."

Celia clutched Hannah's arm. "Hannah, what's going on? Tell me, please. I'd like to help you if I can."

Laughing, Hannah looked at her like she was deranged. "How could you help me? You're even more naive than I was." Then she sobered and shook her head. "Oh God. I shouldn't even be talking to you here. If Marc found out... Come on. Let's go back out and mingle. Forget everything I said."

Celia held back, causing Hannah to stop and look at her. "Hannah..." She bit her lip, then decided to take a major chance. She had no idea when she'd get another opportunity to talk to Hannah alone. "What if I told you I could help you? What if I told you I spoke with your mother this morning and she cried? She desperately wants you to come home, and she's worried sick."

Taking a stunned step backward, Hannah stared at her. Her face went utterly white and her eyes dilated. Then, as if terrified, she looked around to guarantee their privacy and spoke quickly. "You're crazy. Forget you even saw me, okay? And get out of here while you can."

She turned to leave, and practically ran into Jacobs.

He clutched her arms so hard Celia saw the girl wince. "What are you doing, Hannah? Why do you look so stricken?" His gaze shifted to Celia, whose face was, of course, bright red. "Celia? Is everything okay?"

Suspicion reeked from his tone and Celia knew neither of them were going anywhere until Jacobs was ready to let them go. Her heart raced and her wine-muddled brain worked frantically for an excuse.

Quickly, unwilling to let Hannah get in trouble for her folly, she said, "I'm...well, I'm embarrassed to say. I really hoped Hannah could help without anyone else knowing."

Hannah sucked in a breath. Jacobs's eyes darkened and his expression shifted, turning hard. His smile was stiff. "Tell me what the problem is."

"I can't. I'll feel like a fool."

His grip tightened on Hannah until she gasped and stared at Celia with pleading green eyes.

"Do so anyway," Jacobs said. "I insist."

With her face on fire and a hasty look around, Celia mumbled, "I just started my monthly. Oh I know, it's rotten timing and the absolutely worst kind of luck. But I was hoping Hannah could show me where the bathroom is and help me, well, you know. Find what I need." She peeked up at Jacobs to see a bemused expression on his face.

His hands stopped squeezing Hannah to caress her arms instead. Celia wanted to kill him, knowing how shaken Hannah was by their near miss, knowing he'd meant to affect her in just that way. His intimate hold on the girl now was far more lethal than the physical strength in his hands.

Then Jacobs laughed. "Celia, we're all adults here and I work with women on a daily basis. Really, it's not a problem. I'm sure Hannah can help you out. But hurry. Blair is waiting in the den." His gaze went back to Hannah and there was a distinct warning there. "You'll see that she comes directly to the den?"

Hannah smiled, and she appeared for all the world as carefree as when Celia had first met her moments ago. It was as if the heated, nearly disastrous confrontation had never happened. "We ladies will need just a few moments, then we'll be there. I wouldn't want her to miss anything important."

Jacobs rubbed his chin. "Good." Leaning down, he kissed Hannah on the mouth, proving his possession. Hannah smiled and kissed him back.

As they hurried away, Celia thought she might faint from residual fear. She watched Hannah blink, saw her acceptance replaced with pure hatred and disgust.

Celia had to get her away from here, as soon as humanly possible. And if that meant facing Blair and probable degradation, she could do it.

More than ever, she was determined to save Hannah Barrington.

WAITING WASN'T EASY for Alec; he was more a man of action. His tendency was always direct confrontation. Defeat and remove threats. But that wasn't always legal, and he doubted Celia, or Dane for that matter, would tolerate him taking the law into his own hands right now.

The cell phone sat on the truck seat beside him, and he stared at it, daring it to ring, torn between wanting it to so he could rush in and remove Celia from the brownstone, and hoping she was okay and didn't need him at all.

Memories of long ago flooded in on him, making the air inside the truck too thick and hot to breathe. He didn't want to remember that night, or how badly it had ended. Time had proven him to be a better man, more mentally and physically equipped to handle anything that might come along. He wouldn't make the same mistakes—any of them—again.

Harm wouldn't come to Celia, because he wouldn't let it.

Muscles tight despite the pep talk he'd just given himself, Alec rolled down the window and stared through the darkness with his field glasses, forcefully pushing the oppressing memory away. A guard stood by the gate where Celia had been dropped off in that killer outfit that had almost caused his heart to stop. Another guard waited at the front door.

He had no doubt more loomed around every corner. They were all wired, meaning they could communicate easily with each other.

He had not a single doubt he could get past them all if Celia needed him. But if that situation arose, it didn't bode well for the guards, because he'd protect her at any cost and to hell with what was legal.

A sudden yellow glow flared out over the west side

of the lawn from a large window, drawing his attention. Someone had turned on a light. With the glasses, Alec could see shadows of people moving about in the room, through the open draperies. But the angle wasn't right for him to see much more.

Silently, driven by instincts, he left the truck and went to crouch in a scraggly stand of trees on the side of the road. Given the distance from the house, his all-black attire, and his undetectable movements, the guards would never notice him. Again he put the glasses to his eyes and surveyed the house.

He saw Jacobs first, leaning against a desk and sipping a drink. He was smiling, his expression lurid. A lump formed in Alec's throat and even before he saw her, he knew Celia was in that room, that she was the object of Jacobs's interest. He adjusted his position, his body going taut.

Laughing and holding her arms in the air to do another graceful, dancing turn, Celia passed through his line of vision. Another man followed. Heavyset, like a bulldog, and with a crooked smile and avid stare, he watched Celia as she performed. Something happened that made the man laugh. He reached out, cuddled Celia close to his thick side, and kissed her.

Alec dropped the glasses. His heart raced so fast he almost blacked out, rapidly sucking in lungfuls of heavy, humid air. Leaning against a tree, he squeezed his eyes shut and concentrated on breathing, on regaining control so he didn't rush in and start murdering people. But his time would come. Before this was over, he'd meet that man—Jacobs, too—face-to-face.

Then the law be damned because he would have his retribution.

Knowing she'd been with Raymond was always hard enough. But at least that was a man Celia had chosen for herself, a man she'd gone to willingly. He could deal with that—barely. The savage, nearly overwhelming possession he felt for her tended to shake him up. It wasn't something he was used to, yet the feelings grew stronger every day. He was almost tired of fighting it, but that insidious remorse from long ago lingered in his guts, reminding him to be cautious.

Forcing himself into an almost impossible calm, blanking out the turmoil he suffered over Celia and doing his best to regard her as any other woman, he wiped the sweat from his brow and again picked up the glasses to watch. She giggled and flirted, but somehow she managed to stay out of reach for the next twenty minutes. When she finally tipped her head and made an apologetic face, Alec could read her mind as clearly as if the words were written before him.

Poor thing, she had no reserve left. The game had completely done her in and she looked weary from her soul out. He wanted to remove her from that place, coddle her, protect her. He'd hoped to make love to her tonight, but now he reconsidered. She needed some peace and quiet to recoup. He knew only too well the emotional toll of mingling with the very devils that visited your nightmares.

He'd been there too many times himself not to know.

Celia was making her excuses now, planning her departure. She had to be careful not to give herself away, and she was. Like a pro, she handled herself beautifully and he nearly burst with pride, at the same time swearing to himself that once this was over, he'd never let her get this embroiled in danger again.

He watched the room until everyone had walked out and the light was turned off. Then he crept back to the truck and slid behind the wheel. He wouldn't leave until she did, and it was less than a half hour, that felt like a week, before a cab pulled up to the gate. The guard, using a built-in intercom, made a call to the house and minutes later Jacobs escorted Celia down the walk.

He opened the door of the cab for her, then touched her cheek in a gesture that should have seemed tender but instead seemed predatory. Celia, smiling up at him, said something Alec couldn't hear and climbed into the back of the cab.

Both Alec and Jacobs watched the cab pull away until it was out of sight. With a lift of his hand, Jacobs signalled another man who hurried to a car and immediately tailed her. Alec worked his jaw. Jacobs wasn't taking any chances with his new recruit, which left Alec with two options.

He could either avoid detection by staying away from Celia tonight. Or he could reach her motel room first and already be inside when she got there, so that no one would see him enter.

To him, there was really no choice at all.

CELIA KNEW SHE WAS being followed and she prayed for Alec to be discreet. Would he know about the other car? She had to think he would, considering Dane claimed him to be the very best agent in the business.

Of all the things she'd been through, she couldn't bear it if Alec got hurt. She needed him, but with the tail Jacobs had called on her, it wasn't likely he could get anywhere near her tonight. Her head pounded from stress and too much alcohol, and she felt utterly drained. The cabbie, thankfully, was silent.

Since Jacobs had prepaid, the moment the cab stopped she jumped out and hurried to the stairs leading to her motel room. She didn't want to wait and have a possible confrontation with the thug following her. Her hand shook terribly as she tried to get her key to work, and when the door finally swung open she practically leaped inside and then slammed it behind her. With numb, shaking fingers, she turned all the locks on the door.

"Celia."

She screamed, he startled her so badly. But in the next instant she realized it was Alec. She didn't need the light to recognize his voice, his scent, his nearness. Blindly, a sob catching in her throat, she reached out for him. Alec gathered her close, crooning, holding her so tight it should have hurt but instead offered all the comfort she craved. "It's all right now, babe."

She sniffled and tried to collect herself. With a choked laugh, she said, "You're going to think I'm a weenie, carrying on like this."

"No." He chuckled and kissed her forehead.

"You've impressed the hell out of me. How did you get out of there so early?"

She tucked her face under his chin and her shoulders shook with nearly hysterical giggles. "I told Jacobs I had my period."

Alec smiled against her cheek. "Smart."

Pushing back, she cradled his face in her hands. "How did you get here before me?"

"Drove like hell, ran red lights, ignored sirens." He squeezed her. "It was either that or wait till morning because Jacobs had you followed."

"I know. I was afraid you'd...wait."

With each beat of silence that passed, a throbbing thickness filled the air. She could feel Alec's gaze, as tangible as his heat and scent. Then he whispered, "Not a chance."

"Alec..." Suddenly her legs wanted to crumble and Alec lifted her, holding her close while he seated himself on the edge of the bed, holding her in his lap. But she pushed against him, trying to get loose, sudden disgust filling her. "I have to shower. I have to get these awful clothes off, I have to—"

"Shhh..."

"You don't understand." Struggling for breath, pushing as hard as she could against his unbreakable hold, she said, "I... I *do* feel dirty now."

Another beat of silence. "Then we'll both shower." Alec lifted her and carried her into the bathroom.

Celia wondered how he could see so well without a single light on. He must have cat eyes, she thought, then blinked against the harsh fluorescent glare when he turned on the light over the sink.

She didn't want him to see her and she would have turned her back except he didn't let her. "Don't hide from me, honey. Ever."

"But I feel—"

"I know. I understand."

"You can't."

"I do." He bent and pulled her sandals off her feet, tossing them aside. "You feel foul from being near them, letting them think you're like them when you never could be."

Her heart raced, her blood pumped fiercely. "Yes."

After sliding down the side zipper, he skimmed her pants down her legs. "And you want to somehow wash it all away. Believe me, I've done the same too many times to count." Celia knew he spoke to her only as a distraction, but she gratefully accepted it anyway.

She nodded, and Alec's smile was tender.

"Did you find Hannah?" he asked as he slipped her panties down her legs. But Celia was so caught up in the question, she couldn't react to her undressing.

"Oh Alec. It was so awful. If you'd seen her yourself, you wouldn't have a single doubt that she's there against her will. She just doesn't know what to do or where to go."

Alec stood, this time paying no mind to her nudity. He pulled the miniscule crop top over her head and Celia, muffled under the silky material, gasped. She wasn't wearing a bra. Good grief. Alec now had her skinned down to her earrings, and the gold chain around her waist.

He smoothed her tousled hair back into place. "I

believe you, sweetheart. And you'll help Hannah. Everything will work out." He pecked her on the nose before dropping the crop top with the pants.

"Alec..."

He gripped the gold belt and effortlessly snapped the links apart, letting the broken chain join the pile of her clothes. Celia stared at him, gold earrings dangling onto her naked shoulders. Being with Alec this way didn't feel wrong. In fact, it felt incredibly right, the first *right* thing all evening.

Holding his gaze and her breath, she swallowed hard, then reached up and unhooked each earring. Alec took them from her to add to the pile.

"They touched me." The words, so loud in her head, emerged as a faint whisper.

Starting at her ribs, Alec smoothed his hands over her skin, down her belly and back up again, then around and under her arms to coast over her spine. His large hands spanned so much of her on each wide sweep, up and down from shoulders to hips. He tipped up her chin to gaze into her eyes. "Now I've touched you."

Her lip quivered. He was the most miraculous man she'd ever met. "Oh, Alec..."

"Don't you see, honey?" His touch was so gentle, his words more so. "If you weren't discriminating, if you were as *easy* as you say, their attentions would have turned you on. I know every man in there had to enjoy the sight of you, because you're beautiful and sexy and sweet. But that didn't happen, did it? You weren't at all flattered."

Very quietly, she said, "No."

He wasn't through making his point. "You thought you loved Raymond, so he was safe."

She wanted to ask, *What do you think I feel for you?* but she held the words back.

As if he'd read her mind, he said, "You trust me, and you know I respect you, so feeling desire for me isn't something that should shame you. And Celia?" He smoothed back her hair, cupped her face in his palms. "You feel something for me, don't you."

It wasn't a question, but rather a statement of fact, something he seemed supremely sure of. "If you didn't, you wouldn't be so sexually comfortable with me. And I've proven that you are comfortable, haven't I, sweetheart?"

She nodded, still very confused, but also overwhelmed.

Alec sucked in a triumphant breath, his dark eyes glittering. He whispered, "I'll make it better, babe. I promise."

And she knew he could. His touch, burning hot, seemed to penetrate beneath her skin, chasing away all the bad feelings. She shuddered and closed her eyes. "I feel a bit tipsy."

He smiled. "I know. I think you're drunk."

Celia shook her head. "No, not drunk. I know exactly what I'm doing, Alec."

"Don't worry. I'll take care of you."

Her eyes opened. "Will you? Or do you plan to leave me again?"

"Celia—"

Knowing it was a combination of drink, upset

nerves, and relief that for now it was over, she started to hum. Alec's gaze snapped to hers and he stared.

Celia smiled. "I think I have a lot in common with Thelma Houston."

"Who?" Then he shook his head, his gaze suspicious. "Wait, this isn't another muscle-bound wonderwoman you intend to emulate by lifting weights is it? Because honey, I have to tell you, I like your body exactly as it is."

"You don't know Thelma Houston? Really?" At his blank stare, she said, "No, she's not a wonderwoman. But I do use her music when I exercise. I have all her old disco songs on CD. She keeps me motivated." Celia could hardly believe she was standing naked with Alec Sharpe and explaining such a thing. She grinned.

"You're kidding, right?" His lip curled. "*Disco?*"

Again she started humming, ignoring his rude attitude, building up, and her body swayed just a bit. Then, out of the blue, she sang softly, "*Ahhhhh, baby!*"

Alec jumped, then took a step back, hands propped on his hips, a bemused expression on his face.

Celia, not about to let him get away this time, swayed a little closer. She felt giddy and daring and horribly in love, though she wouldn't admit that to Alec. He didn't want her love, but he did want *her*, and she was more than ready for him. She needed him, so his teasing was at an end, whether he liked it or not.

Very low, she sang, "*You started this fire down in my soul—*"

"Celia..."

She kept singing.

"Celia!" Laughing, Alec picked her up and swung her in a circle. "You can stop serenading me."

She cupped his cheeks, so pleased to see his rare laughter, so stunned by his masculine beauty. Loving him so much hurt, but it also made her feel whole and safe. And special.

"The song is called, 'Don't Leave Me This Way.'" She kissed him softly. "You're ready to succumb to my feminine wiles now? Because I want you, Alec Sharpe. I really do." She touched his mouth. "Please, don't leave me this way."

Very gently, he stood her back on her feet and his hands left her. Still with a crooked, immeasurably appealing grin, he began stripping away his own clothes.

Alec was totally unselfconscious in his nudity, kicking off his boots, pushing his jeans down without haste or hesitation. Just looking at him, solid and strong and real, made her feel better. When he was completely naked, he turned to the tub and started the shower. Steam billowed out.

He reached a hand toward her and Celia took it. They stepped into the shower together.

9

ALEC COULDN'T RECALL ever being so charmed, or so turned on, in his life. No woman had ever sung to him—if you could call Celia's slightly off-key, tipsy crooning a song. He wasn't familiar with the singer or the lyrics, but then music had never played a big part in his life, and he couldn't recall ever singing a note. Especially not disco.

On rare occasions he'd listened to a little jazz. On very rare occasions. Fifteen years ago, he could remember coming home to the swelling sounds of a jazz band while Marissa danced around the floor, entertaining herself. He'd be dog-tired, sweaty from a long day of working in the sun, and she'd greet him with a swirl of her skirts and a huge smile, ready to take him to bed and ease his aches and pains. It had taken little more to make him content back then.

But the smiles and the greetings hadn't lasted for long.

Alec realized later that it hadn't been the music, so much as her happiness, that he had been drawn to. He'd fed off it like a starving man. Since then, he hadn't had much reason, or any burning inclination, to listen to music.

Music sort of went hand in hand with partying and a carefree attitude, and he'd sure as hell never been the type to enjoy crowds, raucous laughter, or frivolity.

But Celia obviously was. And he had a feeling his recent show of sexual restraint had something to do with her dredging up that specific tune. *Don't leave me this way*? He smiled. It wasn't exactly a subtle hint, but then Celia wasn't exactly a subtle woman, not where he was concerned.

But none of that mattered now. He had Celia naked, all soft and warm and ready, and his waiting was at an end. He hurt with wanting her from the top of his head down to his big feet with highly concentrated places in-between, and now the only thing holding him back was a desire to make it last a nice long time, the whole damn night if possible.

She tried to face him, but he turned her so her back nestled his chest and the spray from the shower could wash over her breasts. Her nipples peaked and her thighs tightened. She was so hot she made him feel like a horny kid again, ready to explode over just a look. "Let me take care of you first, honey, okay?"

She surprised him by whispering, "Anything you want, Alec."

Damn. Words like that could well push him over the edge. Her body trembled and he knew she was already aroused, which had a similar cause and effect on him. Her body was perfect to him, soft and feminine, but lightly muscled. He thought of the exercise equipment strewn around the floor of her room and he hugged her tighter. She never ceased to surprise him.

In a low rumble, he said, "Relax against me so I can suds you up."

She tipped her head back to see him. "Take your hair out of the ponytail first. I want to see it."

Alec surveyed her curious expression. His hair was long out of disinterest, not out of any need to make a fashion statement. When he worked, as he had tonight, he tied it back to keep it from interfering with his vision. Practicality drove him, not fashion.

But from the day he'd met her, Celia had been fascinated by his lack of social conformity. Her brother was polished; hell, her whole family was polished, down to designer shoes and two-hundred-dollar haircuts that made certain not a single curl strayed out of place. Celia's own hair was usually in a sleek, sophisticated pageboy, but since going undercover, she'd worn it various ways, and he admired her new vamp persona.

If she liked his hair, then he was more than willing to oblige her. He reached back and pulled the band loose. His hair, now long enough to hang to his shoulders, fell free, and Celia gave him a dazed, hot look. "I like it. It makes you look savage, especially with the earring."

Alec grinned again. He had her naked in the shower, both of them strung tight on desire, and they were carrying on a conversation about his hair. "I like *you*. Now hold still while I attend to certain things."

With his hands soapy, he began washing her, starting with her shoulders and upper chest, bypassing her sensitive breasts, regardless of how she squirmed and tried to get his hands to slick over there. He had to go carefully or it'd be done with before he even got started. He'd wanted her so long, fantasized about this for what seemed like forever, that his control was precarious at best. He should have been concerned that she might not be thinking clearly; she'd had a rather eventful night and obviously too much to drink.

But strangely, he *knew* this to be the right decision, for both of them. And truth to tell, he simply wanted her too much to be swayed by scruples he couldn't even pretend to possess.

Washing her slender thighs, he whispered, "Open your legs."

She whimpered softly, but complied. Alec slipped his hands over her, brushing his fingers through her soft intimate curls, letting the rough touch of his callused fingertips mingle with the tantalizing spray from the shower. Celia arched a little, pressing back against him. Her sweet breasts, glistening with water, rose and fell as she struggled for composure; her breathing accelerated, her hands dug into his naked thighs. She was already so close, and he pushed her, his fingers finding a rhythm and stroking deep over slick, tender, swollen flesh.

"I want to kiss you, Alec!"

Heat washed over him, he was so pleased with her. She didn't want to reach her peak without him, afraid, he was certain, that he'd leave her again. He turned her, cradling her shoulders, and kissed her deeply. Against her lips, he explained, "I want you to come now for me, honey, because the devil knows once I get inside you, I won't be able to last long."

She groaned and one small hand slid down his chest to his erection.

Alec sucked in a breath. "That's not going to help, babe."

"We have to be fair," she whispered, looking at him through dazed golden eyes. Her makeup was washed away, her fair hair slicked back by the shower, emphasizing the fine, delicate bones of her face. Her lips were swollen, her cheeks flushed with desire. She was by far the most appealing woman he'd ever seen.

She smiled at him. "You're so gorgeous, Alec, so lean and hard and long-limbed. I probably shouldn't tell you this, but I think about touching you all the time."

He laughed, a little taken aback by her compliment. "I'm not exactly handsome, Celia." He knew, if anything, it was his look of menace that drew women, not classic good looks.

She kissed his chest, his throat, all the time holding him in her small palm, not moving, just holding him, making him crazed. He had to fight the instinct to move his hips, to thrust through her fingers.

"You're rough and dangerous and sinfully sexy. No woman could resist you. I used to feel guilty for wanting you so much." She peeked up. "For all the lurid thoughts I had."

Catching her wrist, he pulled her hand away and pinned it behind her back, which pressed her plump breasts to his ribs. He could feel her stiff little nipples, sliding against his slick wet skin, and adding to his sexual frenzy. When she reached for him with her other hand, he captured it as well, twining his fingers with hers. "You sure as hell held off long enough." The words were low, growled. "Do you have any idea how crazy you make me?"

She squirmed against his tight hold. "Alec, I need you now."

Every time she said it, she drove him closer to the edge. Through gritted teeth, he asked, "Do you still feel dirty, Celia?"

"No." Her wet, naked body writhed against him.

"Are you sure you want me? 'Cause, babe, this won't be a one-time deal. It's going to take a hell of a lot for me to get my fill of you."

Nuzzling against his chest, she found his nipple and licked delicately. "You can take all the time you need."

His control snapped. He released her and within two minutes had finished bathing and rinsing himself. Celia watched, touching him, exploring his body each time he moved. He turned the water off and jerked the shower curtain open. Celia, with a smug, very feminine smile, reached for a towel.

"To hell with that." He picked her up, dripping wet, and walked to the bed.

Now she laughed as he stepped over and around exercise equipment. "Alec, we'll ruin the sheets!"

He didn't bother to answer her as he laid her among the tangle of bedclothes, then went back into the bathroom to fetch his wallet from his jeans. He tossed it onto the nightstand, coming down beside her at the same time and immediately catching a soft breast in his palm. His mouth closed over her nipple, sucking strongly, and Celia gasped. One hand tangled in his hair while her other hand gripped his shoulder, her nails stinging. Licking water from her chest he tasted every inch of her upper body, pausing often to sate himself on her luscious little breasts. Her nipples were rosy, tight, and he couldn't get enough. He thought he might be going too fast, but he wanted to devour her, to devastate her as much as he felt devastated.

When he slipped one hand over her soft belly and thrust two fingers in her, she cried out. She was wet and so damn hot he couldn't wait. His hand moved easily, readying her further, preparing her for him. He felt her muscles clamp down on his fingers, at the same time she moaned.

Cursing, he shoved himself to her side and frantically groped around on the nightstand for his wallet. Celia came to her knees, hugging him from behind, making it more difficult than it should have been to find a condom. When he finally had it on, he flipped her to her back, hooked her legs through his elbows and opened her completely.

She didn't object; her head was back, her eyes closed and her breath came fast and uneven.

Alec slowed, leaning forward by small degrees and watching as his erection pushed into her, past her soft, pink folds. He groaned. *"Celia."*

Her eyes opened, the hazel like warm gold, her pupils dilated. Her cheeks and breasts were warmly flushed and her body trembled beneath him.

"Look at me, babe."

She did, panting in tune to Alec's thundering heart.

Their gazes locked. "Tell me you want this, that you want me."

Her fingers knotted fretfully in the sheets and she licked her lips. Her entire body was tight, straining. Alec pushed in a little deeper. He tortured them both, but it was the most sensational thing he'd ever felt.

"I want you, Alec," she groaned, her voice raw and filled with need. "I've wanted you for such a long time." Panting, her hands smoothed over her breasts, as if appeasing an ache, and Alec lost it. Seeing her touch herself was like throwing gasoline on a live fire—instant combustion.

With a harsh growl, he buried himself inside her, forcing his way past the slight natural resistance of her body. Stilling, he dropped forward and they both moaned. Celia locked her legs around him and Alec pressed his face to her throat, smelling the sweet scent of her body, her hair, of Celia. *Too good*, he thought, *too damn good*. Making a quick adjustment, he put one hand beneath her hips and lifted her so she could take all of him and at that moment, she came, shocking the hell out of him and pushing him over the edge.

Her body arched so hard she lifted him from the bed. He thrust just as hard, pinning her down again.

He could feel the clenching of her inner muscles, the slight sting of her nails, and again, her sharp little teeth. He shouted, the pleasure was so acute, and with every muscle straining, he buried himself in her again and again, then joined her, coming until he felt too sated, too incredibly weak, to draw another single breath.

He rested there on her, trying to gather his scattered wits and reconcile how incredible it felt to make love to Celia Carter. He'd known it would be good—knowing had kept him awake many nights and reduced him to an animal on the prowl. But he hadn't expected this, something more than mere sex, something beyond the physical. He didn't like it, but didn't quite know what to do about it.

Her rapid breaths still fanned his ear, and her gentle hands coasted up and down the long length of his damp back. He wanted to shout that he didn't need her comfort, her gentleness, not after she'd so physically satisfied him. But the words wouldn't come. He could barely draw breath. He felt her hesitate, then touch his right biceps.

"Alec?" She spoke softly, breathlessly. "Where did you get the tattoo?"

He closed his eyes. Maybe she'd think he was asleep. Maybe she'd even think he'd died, which actually had been a pretty close thing judging by the furious drumming of his heart and the lack of coordination in his limbs. But his luck wasn't that great.

She tightened her hold, giving him a full body hug, then asked, "Alec?"

He sighed, resigned. Well damn. Bliss can't ever last for more than a few minutes.

Alec pushed up to his elbows. Celia looked so sweet with her wet hair tangled, her cheeks still warm. Almost against his will, he kissed her gently, and he never wanted to stop kissing her. That made him frown as he pulled away. "My wife talked me into it. Fifteen years ago."

Her eyes widened and her face went pale. "You have a wife?"

Rolling to his back and propping his arms behind his head, he stared at the ceiling. Light from the bathroom cast long shadows and showed a fading watermark directly over his head.

He'd known, sooner or later he'd have to tell her if he slept with her. Not that she needed an entire accounting of his life, no one did. But intimacy in the sack brought about other intimacies. And Celia was a curious woman, always digging in where she shouldn't be. If the situation were reversed, if she'd tried to hide aspects of her life rather than presenting herself as an open book, he'd already have gotten into her personal file at Dane's office, or he'd have run a check on her. But Celia wasn't a natural snoop, and the thought never would have occurred to her to invade his privacy.

One reality touched his tired brain: knowing would likely disgust her and put the distance he needed back between them. Not a physical distance, because he planned to keep her right where she was until he got the ache out of his system and could think rationally again. But the emotional distance was something he needed, and knowing a bit about his past ought to accomplish it. That alone was reason enough to tell her.

He sighed again, then said with no emotion, no inflection whatsoever, "Not any more. She's dead."

Alec had half expected her to leap from the bed, or to curse him. Knowing Celia, he'd definitely expected some sort of volatile reaction. All he got was a heavy silence that felt like an anvil sitting on his windpipe, before she turned and cuddled up at his side. Surprised, he hesitated, then put one arm around her and prayed she wouldn't start crying. He really hated it when she cried.

"Did you love her?"

Alec stilled. Shit, he hated questions like that. He'd rather deal with a tear or two. "Celia..."

"You must have," she whispered, her voice low and reverent, filled with tenderness, "to put something permanent on your body." With one finger, she lightly traced the faded heart on his arm. "Right here, where the color's kind of smudged...did you have her name removed?"

Her name, but the memory had lingered, so overall it'd been a wasted effort. "Yeah."

"Why didn't you have the whole thing taken off?"

He glanced down at her. Her bare body curled against his, one slender thigh over his thicker, hairier one, her belly pressed up against his hip. Her skin was so fair against his darker body. He felt the renewed stirrings of desire and wanted to end the conversation as quickly as it had started.

With a hot look, he told her, "It hurt like hell, having the thing lasered off, so I took off what I had to and figured to hell with the rest." As a warning he added, "No one ever asks me about it."

"Why did you have to have her name taken off?"

He looked away in disgust, his temper starting on a low boil. Celia heeded his warnings with as much caution as the wall might. "Look, Celia, why don't we talk about this some other time?"

"Because I know you won't. Please, Alec?"

Damn, he both hated and loved the way she asked him so nicely whenever she really wanted something. Her softly spoken words had the effect of bringing his body to full attention; there was no way she could miss his blatant erection.

She didn't. Her hand crept down his belly, stroking the line of dark hair there, paused to toy with his navel for an excruciating moment, then continued on until she curled her small fist around him. His stomach muscles felt like iron, he was strung so taut.

Without inhibition, she explored him, softly cupping his testicles, petting his rigid length, letting her thumb stroke over the very tip of him... Alec ground his teeth together. *Talk about torture...*

"All right. I had her name taken off right after she died because I... Well..."

It wasn't like him to stumble over his words and he resented her for making him do so now. He turned, grabbed both her hands and pinned them over her head. Looming over her, his frown fierce, he barked, "So you want all the gory details, do you?" Her eyes widened, and she held her breath. "All right."

Celia bit her bottom lip. "Alec—"

"My wife was the town slut." He stared down at her, refusing to let her look away. She'd pushed for details and now she could just deal with them. "Like most guys ruled by hormones, the first time I got laid, I stupidly mistook lust for love."

He had to laugh at his own idiocy. Telling Celia about it should have made him uncomfortable, but their circumstances—naked in a bed after having just made love—superseded all other emotion. He wanted the telling through so he could have her again. And again and again, until the wanting went away. He didn't like wanting her; anytime he'd wanted someone, it had ended up hurting like hell. His jaw locked with that pathetic thought and self-loathing filled him. He was a grown man now, and he'd long since learned to take life for what it was, without the illusions. Maybe it was time Celia learned, too.

"I'd had a less than sterling home life after my mother died of ovarian cancer. My old man had run off on us when I was just a little kid, so my grandfather ended up with me. The old guy tried, I'll give him that, but we didn't have much in the way of luxury, and I was already mad as hell at the world. I didn't make things easy on him. Whenever I'd push him too hard—and I was always real good at pushing—he'd get out a birch rod. The old coot had a hell of a swinging arm."

Big, horrified tears welled up in Celia's eyes and Alec shook her, saying through his teeth, "Don't you dare cry for me, Celia. I never got a damn thing that I didn't deserve. Except maybe my wife."

Celia started to speak, but he didn't want to hear anything she had to say. Knowing Celia and her soft heart, she'd try pitying him first, then cajoling, then comfort. He didn't want any of it. He wanted to be inside her again so he could forget everything else in the explosive pleasure.

Loosening his hold on her arms, he said, "She had a similar background to mine, but with her, it was a stepfather to contend with, a real mean son of a bitch that I used to dream about punching out. Of course I never did, but the fantasy was sweet. And if he hadn't run off when he did, I might have eventually gone after him. Marissa celebrated with me the day he skipped town. She dragged me down by the river and went wild over me. That was the first night we had sex.

"I rebelled over my life by being a jerk, but Marissa rebelled by taking any kind of *love* she could get, from any guy who'd give it. I felt sorry for her at first, because she was one pathetic kid, then lovestruck after she gave me my first taste of a female's body. She was experienced enough to know exactly what she was doing, and with almost no effort, she turned me inside out. I let her become my whole focus. I thought she'd change, that I could make her life happy again, that she'd be content just being with me."

He laughed, the sound a little too raw for his liking. "Turned out I was just one more guy in a long line of idiots."

Celia turned her head to stare at the tattoo, the tears now clinging to her lashes. She gave a small, delicate sniff as she fought off the tears, but otherwise was quiet. Alec guessed she'd gotten more in the way of a story than she'd bargained for. He hadn't intended to go into so much detail. The words had just sort of come out, against his will.

He brushed her tears away with his thumbs, then continued. "As soon as we graduated high school, I started making plans for us to get married. I got a job working a construction site, saved as much money as

I could, and right before we turned nineteen, we eloped. To me, to the young stupid kid I was back then, that marriage was forever."

Celia's eyes searched over his face, intent and filled with sadness. "Because you loved her."

His laugh was genuine this time. "Love? I don't think so, babe. Hell, no nineteen-year-old knows what he's thinking or feeling, especially when he's only thinking with his gonads and not his brains. I thought I could make a difference, thought I could *save* her. But she straightened me out quick enough. Like your little Hannah, she wanted fame and fortune real bad. She was always talking about us moving away, but I could barely keep us afloat, much less consider packing up and heading out.

"One day I came home from a twelve-hour shift to find a note saying she'd gone to visit a friend in Chicago. It wasn't until the next day that I found out she'd emptied out the savings account, not that we had much, but it would have been enough to pay the bills that were due. I had no idea where she'd gone, or where to find her. It took me awhile to track her down and by the time I caught up to her a couple of months later, she was strung out on dope and didn't hesitate to tell me she liked the city life a lot more than anything I could offer her."

He got quiet, remembering despite himself. With the memory came the feelings of helplessness, of betrayal. They'd buried themselves deep in his soul and he'd never been able to shake them off. Celia touched his jaw and he admitted, "She was living with three people—two of them men."

Pressed up against him so tightly, Alec felt her quickly drawn breath, the way she stiffened. "Oh no. Alec, what did you do?"

He grinned evilly. "I beat the hell out of both the guys, though I had no idea which one was for her. Hell, maybe they both were. Knowing how insatiable she always was, I wouldn't have put it past her. The cops got called, I got arrested, and she told me she was going to file for a divorce. I felt so damn sick, I didn't even care. Right then, at that moment, standing in that crowded police station knowing all those uniforms felt sorry for me and that they were thinking what an ass I was to have ever fallen for her in the first place, I almost wanted to kill her myself. I did tell her to stay the hell out of my life."

Celia wrapped her arms tight around him in a near choke hold. "She was wrong, Alec. But don't you see? She didn't know any better—"

"Like your Hannah?" He grabbed her arms to pull her loose, but she was like a damn spider monkey, clinging tight.

"No!" Celia leaned back to look in his eyes, but didn't loosen her hold on him. He didn't want to hurt her, so he had to give up on prying her loose and let her squeeze on him all she wanted. "Hannah wants help, Alec. She's not like that. Her circumstances didn't drive her away, only her bad judgment did."

"Don't worry, sweetheart." He gave her a twisted smile that he knew damn good and well wouldn't reassure her one bit, but it was the best he could offer at the present. "Just because I couldn't do a damn thing for my wife doesn't mean I'll leave little Hannah behind. You and I made a deal, and I'll hold up my end of the bargain. I just wonder if she'll thank you in the end."

His cold tone must have disturbed her, for she shivered and said, "Alec? What happened to your wife? You told me she died."

"Yeah." He removed every bit of inflection he could from his tone, not wanting to give anything away, not wanting her pity, or even her understanding. "One month after I walked away without even trying to bring her home, she died. Overdosed during a party with her upscale friends. She never did get that divorce, so they called me, and when I went to see her body..."

His voice trailed off and he closed his eyes, but he could still plainly see her, how ravaged she'd looked, how thin and old. *Jesus.* Her life in the big city had taken its toll. And Alec had never quite forgiven himself for not trying harder to bring her around. It had seemed from the time she was born, she hadn't had a snowball's chance in hell of surviving. Like so many other people, he'd just given up on her. No matter what he told Celia, no matter what excuses he had, he'd let her down.

He knew now he'd never loved her, but he had felt sorry for her and he still did. He'd had a responsibility to her, one that he'd conveniently forgotten when his pride got bruised. Some days he felt so guilty he could taste it.

In so many ways, he felt sorry for Hannah, too, for being gullible and naive and vulnerable. But he didn't want to get involved again. He hadn't saved his wife, so why should he save anyone else? If it weren't for Celia insisting... He hadn't realized his arms had tightened on Celia again until she moved.

She kissed him. "Shhh. I'm sorry I made you dredge that all up."

"I was behind on all my bills after the money she'd taken. I was barely able to catch up, and then she died and I couldn't afford a funeral. My grandfather didn't have any money, and her mother couldn't have cared less. She was off with a new man by then." He closed his eyes. "I had to let the state bury her..."

"Alec." Celia kissed him, giving him so much in the touch of her mouth to his.

In near desperation, Alec cupped her face, holding her still while he took over, while he kissed her hungrily. Celia made him feel stronger and weaker than any other person he'd known. She stole his strength, but gave it back to him in spades.

He opened his mouth against her neck, drawing the skin in against his teeth, moving his mouth down to suck voraciously at her nipples. She groaned, surprised at his urgency, but still responsive as ever. He muttered, his tone thick and dark, "Just give me this, Celia. It's all I want. Just this..."

For an answer, she wrapped her soft slender thighs tightly around his waist—and he was a goner.

He didn't believe in love; what he'd felt for his wife hadn't even been real, but more a pathetic effort to save her and himself, an effort he'd failed miserably. There hadn't been another soul alive he'd let get under his skin since then. He saved people as part of his job. They were simple assignments, nothing more, easy to work through, easy to forget. Hannah could have been an assignment for someone else so he wouldn't have had to get involved.

But now there was Celia. And truth was, she scared him half to death.

Making love to her seemed his only option, a physical way to drown out the sentient turmoil she caused. And now that he'd had release, just a bit of the edge was gone and he could take his time.

Alec did all the things to her he'd ever imagined, and she revelled in each and every one. He made love to her tenderly, and then with primitive determination, almost violent in his need. But she was with him every step of the way, reacting just as explosively, totally uninhibited. Finally, in the wee hours of the morning, they both fell asleep.

Unfortunately, Alec dreamed of his wife, her lush body thin and cold, her sexy features ravaged by death, and somehow her face and Celia's were combined.

And just as he'd failed his wife, he failed Celia. Despite her skewed perspective on things, Alec knew she wouldn't give herself so freely to a man unless she cared, unless she...*loved him*. In a deep part of himself he didn't want to recognize, Alec accepted the truth.

The worst that could happen, had.

10

No AMOUNT of physical exertion could chase away her demons this morning. Celia had already worked up a sweat, pushed herself harder than she ever had before, and all she could think of was last night. It had been both the most wonderful, and the most distressful, night of her life. Alec had loved her in ways she'd only dreamed of, ways that would have shocked her not so long ago, but had seemed incredibly romantic and intimate and special last night. *With Alec.*

He'd also been brutally honest about his views of the world—and she didn't fit into his equation.

Celia had stirred when Alec crawled out of bed early that morning. But she didn't tell Alec she was awake. She wanted time alone to think. She heard him washing up in the bathroom, heard him quietly dressing. When he walked over to her side of the bed, she kept her eyes tightly closed. Regulating her breathing wasn't easy, but she just couldn't face him yet, not knowing what she did now about his past— and how difficult it would be for him to trust in love again. Strangely, he didn't seem to blame his wife or his grandfather or anyone else who'd let him down. He only blamed himself. Her heart wanted to crumble for the hurts he'd been dealt.

His rough, wonderful fingers touched her cheek,

smoothed her hair, and seconds later she heard the soft click of the door as it closed behind him. She knew he'd hesitated, that he'd peeked out to make sure it was clear to leave. He'd broken his own rule about staying over and taking chances, and that, too, would anger him at himself. He'd see it as a lack of responsibility on his part. He was so protective...

The tears had started then. All night she'd held them off, knowing he hated to suffer through her excesses of emotion. But her heart hurt and she wanted so badly to curl up and hide away. Of course she didn't.

Minutes after Alec was gone, she left the bed and found his note claiming he'd be back in the early afternoon. At first she was so relieved to find out he wasn't gone for good. She hadn't been certain about that, not with the way she'd pushed him. Then Celia realized that she hadn't told him about the appointment she had with Marc Jacobs's crony at two o'clock. If Alec didn't make it back in time, he'd no doubt be livid to find her gone. He was overprotective to a fault, did the best he could to shield her, but he didn't love her.

And he never would.

Celia squeezed her eyes shut as she did another series of crunches, working to distract herself, but with no success. Even Thelma Houston singing loudly from the portable CD player couldn't penetrate her clamoring thoughts.

She loved Alec, but he had forever shut himself off from love. She had to accept the facts. Her brother, Dane, had been telling her for some time what a loner

Alec was, how he seemed to thrive on his seclusion. Even Dane's wife, Angel, who Alec adored, made him nervous if she offered him the slightest affection. He approached every job with single-minded, cold deliberation, and an absolute lack of personal involvement that effectively settled things with the least amount of fuss. He didn't want to be involved, not with anyone for any reason.

He'd told her, and his life-style proved it; Alec wanted her for sexual release, but with no ties.

He hadn't been wrong about the chemistry between them. No, she didn't feel used for knowing Alec's touch. She felt cherished, and that hurt more than anything.

His poor wife. To Celia, she'd sounded so sad and misguided. And poor Alec. Despite what he'd said, regardless of how he'd thundered and thumped his chest, he was hurting still, and his guilt had been as plain to her as his smudged tattoo with the name removed.

Celia, already sweating, strained to lift herself one more time on the chin-up bar. To boost herself, she started singing with Thelma, her own rendition of a blood-rushing war cry.

"I'd have thought I exercised you plenty last night."

Celia yelped at the intrusion of that amused, masculine voice. Dropping almost to her knees, she whirled to face Alec. His arms were laden with packages, and there was a wide, taunting smile on his unshaven face.

He looked delicious, she thought, in his rumpled

jeans, dark T-shirt and flannel, like a renegade, lethal and sexy and more than capable of anything he set his mind to. Even though her embarrassment was extreme, she couldn't help admiring him. "Alec, your note said you'd be gone till the afternoon!"

"It is afternoon."

"No, it's only eleven."

He shrugged. "Close enough. I got everything taken care of faster than I expected."

Still struggling with his smile, Alec put the boxes and bags on the small table, never quite taking his gaze from her. Legs braced apart, arms crossed over his chest, he was the perfect picture of the arrogantly amused male.

Celia nervously tugged her T-shirt lower. Other than her panties, it was all she wore, all she ever wore while working out in the oppressive summer heat. She cleared her throat. "Actually, I'm glad you're here."

"Me, too." Stalking forward, his eyes on the damp T-shirt clinging to her breasts, he added, "I expected to find you still in bed, all drowsy and sweet, but maybe this is even better." He glanced up, his gaze holding hers. "You're already...warmed up."

"Alec." Celia held her arms out, warding him off. She needed to talk to him, to explain about her plans with Jacobs, but he easily dodged her resistance and in a single move she found herself flat on the bed and Alec firmly planted between her thighs.

"You smell good," he muttered, nuzzling her shoulder and throat.

"I'm sweaty!"

"Earthy. You smell like a woman. I like it."

"Alec, please, I have to talk to you."

"I love how you say *please* so prettily." He kissed her breast through the cotton, lightly nibbled on her nipple. "It turns me on."

She couldn't help but laugh even as her body softened with wanting him. "I'm finding out that everything turns you on."

"Everything about you. Believe it or not, I have icy cold iron control everywhere else."

"Really?" She knew it to be true at work, but did he mean with other women also? The idea pleased her. If she couldn't have everything, at least she had something special.

Alec started inching her shirt up, and she knew once he had her naked, it'd be all over. She gripped his ponytail, making him wince, and blurted out, "Jacobs set up another meeting for me today."

Alec stilled. "When?"

"At two o'clock."

He stared at her hard for a moment, then shoved himself into a sitting position. Glaring down at where she still lay sprawled on the mattress, he asked, "And you're just now telling me?"

Celia scrambled into a sitting position as well, pulling the shirt over her knees to maintain a false sense of modesty. "Well, last night you didn't exactly give me a chance, now did you?"

He leaned forward, nose to nose with her. "So why didn't you tell me this morning instead of playing possum?"

Celia tucked in her chin. "You knew I was awake?"

Alec rolled his eyes and stood to pace. "All right. From now on, business comes first." He looked at her, his eyes black with inner fire, pinning her. "There's nothing I'd rather do than spend a week in bed with you, but that's going to have to come second to solving this business with Jacobs—if you're still determined to see this through?"

She lifted her chin. "Of course I'm still determined."

He muttered a curse. "That's what I figured."

"You're the one who distracted me last night!"

"And I'll damn well distract you again tonight, and the next night. But from now on, tell me what's going on the minute you see me. No more holding back. What if I hadn't gone shopping this morning? Then we'd be in a hell of a mess."

Celia had no idea what his shopping had to do with her plans for Jacobs. She gave him a blank look and he sighed.

"Celia, I don't want you around Jacobs again without a wire. It's too risky. Watching you from outside that house last night took a good ten years off my life. I don't want to go through that again. Seeing you in there, but not knowing what's going on—anything could happen, and the more we deal with that bastard, the less I like it. The only way I can approve any of this—"

"You can approve!"

"—is if you're wired so I can hear what's going on."

Celia jumped to her feet to face him. Alec was back to his old, stubborn, autocratic self and she wouldn't stand for it. "I thought we'd already decided that I'm going to do whatever I choose, Alec Sharpe! You don't own me."

Propping his hands on his hips and acting totally unaffected by her ire, he said, "If I did, I'd have you on a leash."

She almost exploded with fury, and then somehow, some small niggling suspicion, crept into her brain. Alec wanted her anger. He'd tried jumping her bones the minute he'd come in, which would have, in effect, put her in the place he wanted to keep her: as a mere bed partner, her importance defined by physical activities.

But then she'd told him about Jacobs and his natural protective instincts kicked in. Alec felt a noble, if detached, responsibility for almost everyone, especially people smaller, older, or weaker than himself. But he seemed to take a personal interest in Celia. He always had, almost from day one. Why hadn't she ever made serious note of that before?

Because she'd always been too busy fighting off her own attraction for him.

Now she no longer wanted to fight, and she was seeing things much more clearly. Watching him warily, she said, "You're being a jerk, Alec."

"Because I don't want to see you raped by that bastard?"

"No." She shook her head, shaken by his words despite her false bravado. "I accept your concern because I believe it's genuine."

He smirked. "Gee, thanks."

"But it's your attitude that needs work." She narrowed her eyes and looked him over, unsure how far she should push. But this was important. She loved him, and even if he never loved her back, she wanted him to accept that love existed, and that he, especially, was a very worthy man to receive it. "Last night you weren't so obnoxious. You were...understanding, when I first came in."

He laughed. "Last night you were all but falling apart. I don't kick anyone when they're down, especially not a lady I want to get intimate with."

Oh God. He was going for the jugular today. Feeling her resolve weaken, Celia lifted her chin. "I thought you were kind and considerate because you cared about me."

Alec stepped closer, his gaze predatory. "Oh, I do care, honey. But don't give me that doe-eyed innocent look, like you think I should be pledging love everlasting just because we rocked the earth in bed."

Very quietly, she whispered, "I never thought that, Alec."

"Good. Because what we have together is too damn hot to start watering down with false expectations."

"Sex?"

"Damn right. Sensational sex, from both our perspectives, and I've got your claw marks all over me to prove it."

She almost hit him. The air left her in a whoosh and she felt herself folding in, closing down. She couldn't banter with him, not when he was intent on forcing an ugly void between them. Turning, she headed for the bathroom, wanting only an escape, but Alec wrapped one steely arm around her waist, drawing her up short. A physical battle would be beyond stupid; the man was hard as granite whereas she was still trying to develop a little muscle tone. She waited to see what he would do, but he merely held her, pulling her tight against his chest.

She felt his indecision like a tangible thing, pulsing over her, and then his mouth touched her temple, her ear. "Where are you going, babe?"

Celia held herself perfectly still, afraid she'd fall apart and start crying if she moved a single muscle. Not only would she refuse him the satisfaction of winning, her pride demanded she hold tough, that she prove herself capable of dealing with anything he dished out. "I need to shower and get ready."

"Not yet."

"Alec..." She squeezed her eyes shut. If he said one more hurtful thing to her now, she might not be able to forgive him.

But he simply held her. "We have things to talk about, and I brought you something to eat."

"I'm not hungry."

"You'll eat anyway."

Shoving out of his arms, she faced him again and said, "Get it through your thick head, Sharpe! You're not my keeper."

Eyes glinting, he leaned against the wall and folded his arms over his chest. She recognized that now as his arrogant stance, and she braced herself.

"But I am." The words were soft, satisfied. "Don't you remember our little arrangement? I'd stay and help you save Hannah, and you'd give me..." He shrugged. "...anything I want. Right now, I want you to stop running away from me."

Her hands fisted at his fickle attitude. "Then stop trying to drive me away. It's not even necessary. Believe me, Alec, I already figured out where I stand. And I'm not so naive that I have illusions of a lasting love." Bitterness, heartache, threatened to choke her, but she added, "Not with you."

That gave him pause. He pushed away from the wall and paced. Hands on hips, his head dropped forward, he stared at the floor for several moments in a pose of indecision and frustration. Celia could almost feel him thinking, an angry, fretful process, before he finally looked at her again. "Fair enough." He searched her face silently, then shook his head. "Now sit. I really do need to talk to you."

Damned pigheaded man. "Alec, that was only marginally nicer than a dog's command."

He smiled. "I'm sorry. Would you please sit down so I can instruct you on the finer points of a wire, since you'll definitely be in possession of one before you go anywhere near Jacobs or his cronies again."

"Is there time?" She glanced at the clock. "I have to be there in just a few hours."

"Be where, exactly?" he asked, as she seated herself at the tiny, scarred table.

Celia winced. "I gather it's a studio of sorts. I'm supposed to do a...a photo shoot."

Alec closed his eyes, a sure indication that he didn't exactly like what she'd just told him. "And you agreed to do this without even discussing it with me first?"

"Oh, right. What was I supposed to do, Alec? Tell Jacobs's friend, 'Oh excuse me, please, but I have to ask my private eye pal if it's okay?' Get real."

"I'm not your damn *pal*, Celia."

"Don't I know it!"

He gave her a look that said she was pushing it, but kept his calm. "Okay, start over. Who is Jacobs's friend, where are you going, and who will be there?"

Well, shoot. This was going to be the tricky part. She hadn't expected Alec to be in such a rotten mood when she told him. "Jacobs has this friend, Blair Giles, who's supposedly a photographer, but Hannah told me while we were in the bathroom, that he's a really nasty sort. She said Jacobs uses him to weed out the girls. If anyone balks at working with Giles, Jacobs drops them as being too risky and too much trouble. So you see, I *had* to do this, Alec. If I hadn't agreed, they'd have been onto me and I wouldn't even have the chance to talk to Hannah again."

Alec leaned back and crossed his ankles. He was too rock steady for nervous movements, but his hands gripped the edge of the table, giving away his anxiety. "Sounds like you and little Hannah had quite a chat. If she wants to be saved, why didn't she just agree to it then?"

Celia measured her words carefully, unsure of how to convince him. "Yes, we did talk some. But she was too afraid to trust me beyond a few warnings." Celia told him all about her close call with Jacobs and how he'd treated Hannah, how pale and afraid the girl had been afterward. "It was awful, Alec. When we got in the bathroom, she was too scared to listen to much I had to say, and definitely too afraid to linger long enough to give me a chance to convince her. All she wanted to do was warn me."

"About Jacobs?"

Nodding, she said, "Yeah, and this Giles fellow. She told me the only way around him is to not act afraid. He... I guess he sort of likes it when he can scare a woman or make her nervous."

Alec's entire countenance tightened until he was suddenly on his feet, standing over Celia. "Don't go."

Her heart swelled. He could pretend what was between them was only sexual, but the heat in his eyes now told a very different story. Like a battered child, he was wary of caring too much for anyone, shying away from tenderness—or love. She didn't fool herself into thinking she could have his love, not when he guarded it so closely. But she still wanted to give him hers. Alec deserved that much, and more.

Touching his jaw with a gentle hand, she said, "I'm not her, Alec."

He backed up, his gaze diamond hard, but also a bit panicked. "Besides being melodramatic, what the hell is that supposed to mean?"

Celia stood and walked to him until she could wrap her arms around his waist. He was warm and hard and touching him made her feel more alive than she'd thought possible. "I didn't have a tragic childhood. I'm not naive or desperate. And I'm smart. I can take care of myself, Alec, and while I'm there, I'll have you to help me. It'll be okay."

For the longest time Alec was stiff, his arms hanging at his side. She knew he was struggling, but in the end, he wrapped her close and rocked her in his arms. "I know you're not dumb, Celia. Far from it. But you're out of your element here."

"And that's why you're helping." She leaned back and smiled at him. "For a price, as you so rudely reminded me."

"Celia..."

"Which," she added, interrupting him, "I'll expect to have to pay as soon as I get home tonight."

His gaze softened and he looked down at her breasts in the clinging cotton. She jumped slightly when his warm palms slid to her barely clad fanny, cuddling her closer. "Is that right? Am I to understand that you'll willingly be at my mercy?"

"Very willingly," she whispered.

His gaze shot to her face, suddenly fierce, and very possessive. Celia shivered, and cleared her throat. Teasing Alec was like tugging on the tiger's tail—exciting, but also a little nerve-wracking. "Where is this wire going to be?" she asked, quickly changing the subject and hoping to distract him. "I don't have to hide it anyplace...*risqué*, do I?"

He laughed, as she had known he would, but it was more a concession to her, an effort to lighten the mood, than in any real humor. "No, if we put it anyplace that muffled it too much, I wouldn't be able to hear a damn thing." Then he smacked her bottom. "Not to mention how uncomfortable it might be for you."

His wicked grin had her smiling too. "Well, thank goodness for that."

Alec released her. "It's lucky for you I went shopping today, though I was thinking more about the night to come at the bar than anything going on this afternoon. I hated not being able to hear what Jacobs said to you, especially when you started dancing around him."

"He'd just asked me to pose."

"And of course you jumped to obey."

"Of course." Then she added, "Actually I was afraid he'd ask me into the back room to do it or something, so instead I jumped the gun and did it right there, in front of everyone. It was horribly embarrassing."

"But you're right, it was better than being alone with him."

She shrugged. "I thought so."

Alec shook his head. "Well, along with food, I picked up a small detecting device that no one will notice as long as you don't advertise it. But I won't even put it directly on you. That's too risky. I was thinking maybe your purse, if you think you can keep it with you all the time."

"Of course."

Alec reached for a bag and dumped out the contents. Besides some things she didn't recognize, he had a fresh box of condoms—which made her cheeks bloom with renewed color—and a very ordinary-looking pen. He held it out to her. "Here you go."

Celia blinked. "What am I supposed to do with that?"

"Keep it close. It's your bug."

"You're kidding?" She touched the ballpoint tip

and got a speck of ink on her finger. "It's just a regular pen."

"No, it just looks like a regular pen, but it has a hidden transmitter. That little baby will pick up a whisper forty feet away and it transmits up to five hundred meters with respectable quality, which means I won't have to be too damn close, but I sure as hell intend to be close enough to get you out of there if any trouble starts."

Alec took it from her when she started to inspect it too closely. "Let's not break it, okay? They don't come cheap." He shook his head at her, then reached for her small bag. "If you clip it high on the inside like this, and leave your purse open, we shouldn't have any problems."

She was really impressed. "Wherever did you find it?"

He snorted. "In a town this size? There must be at least a hundred commercial outlets, though I got that one from an underground source."

"Just like that?"

"Celia, I couldn't drive down the block without picking up a couple dozen eavesdropping devices on a scanner. The world is not as pretty, or as secure, as you like to think."

She ignored his continued references to her naiveté. "So how do we know Jacobs doesn't have a bug in here somewhere?"

"Because no one's been in here or I'd know about it. Believe it or not, I do pay attention."

Celia shrugged. "Okay, so you're Super Sleuth. Forgive my doubting tendencies."

"Smart-ass."

"Sorry." She grinned, showing she really wasn't the least bit contrite.

"Celia, you do have to be careful what you say around Hannah. I doubt Jacobs spends the money to bug the girls, because he strikes me as the type to be overly confident in his domination. But be careful all the same, all right?"

Celia nodded, a little overwhelmed by the possibility that any conversation she had might be listened to. With a definite edge of sarcasm, she said, "This is just great, Alec. I feel better about the whole thing already."

A slight smile tugged at his sensual mouth. "Yeah, well don't get too cocky on me. I still don't like this setup worth a damn, and from now on, don't even think about accepting any dates without running it past me first." When she started to object again, he shushed her with a finger pressing on her lips. "I mean it, Celia. Make up any damn excuse you want, tell him you'll have to call him after you free up some time, but no more without me approving it first. Got that?"

She nodded grudgingly. Now that she understood him a little better, she didn't mind his autocratic attitude nearly as much.

Not that she'd let him boss her around, but...

"Now," he said, pulling her into his arms once again. "I've held off as long as I can. You prancing around here like that is making me crazy." His voice dropped and he nuzzled her ear. "I need you, Celia."

Already her skin tingled and her stomach did flips.

The way he'd said that had sounded like so much
more than just sex. She glanced at the clock. It'd be a
rush, but...

"I want you, too, Alec. So much."

The words were no sooner out of her mouth than
she found herself in his arms, on her way to the bed.
Some things were worth making time for.

11

HE'D SCREWED UP royally and he knew it.

Alec, crouched around a corner at the back of the warehouse "studio" where Celia was presently posing, chewed on the inside of his jaw and called himself three kinds of a fool. He'd distracted her, ruining her focus, and then sent her to her destination running late, which had made her frazzled. Whether or not she'd absorbed his last few warnings of caution and discretion, he couldn't say. After he'd kept her in bed for an hour, exorcising his own private demons on her very willing body, she'd had to fly through her shower, and fixing her hair and makeup. She'd thought the result majorly disappointing.

Alec knew any man looking at her would go nuts.

With her slightly tousled hair, her glowing eyes and cheeks and her kiss-swollen lips, she looked like sensuality incarnate, like a woman made to take a man, and there wasn't a male alive who wouldn't recognize and appreciate the picture she presented.

It was one more thing to put him on edge. The whole setup stunk to high heaven. The "studio" was definitely a facade, more an abandoned warehouse in a not-so-great area where law enforcement didn't make the time to visit with any regularity. The building was old, the brick facing a little rough and dirty in places. Alec had circled the whole building before Celia went in, and on the west side there were even some windows that had been boarded up. It looked as though only part of the warehouse was in use—the part Giles and Jacobs needed to lure in young women.

The blacktop parking lot where Alec crouched was sweltering hot with the midday sun burning down on him. Sweat trickled down his temples and down the small of his back, but he ignored the discomforts, all his focus on Celia and what she was about to do.

Small background noises reached Alec through his receiver as Celia was greeted and walked down a long concrete hallway. He heard the cavernous echoing of her high heels, the sounds of opening and closing doors, then stillness. They'd obviously taken her to a back office.

A male voice intruded, making Alec's senses come alive.

"Ms. Sharpe! You're right on time."

Alec's brows rose. *Ms. Sharpe?* She'd used *his* last name? A grin teased at his mouth until he caught himself and frowned. His instinctive reaction unnerved him, but he didn't have time to ponder the ramifications of it, not when Celia and the man were speaking. He didn't want to miss a single word, though so far the conversation was banal enough. This man, then, wasn't Blair Giles. The voice was young and enthusiastic and slightly flirtatious. Alec could well imagine any young man being enamored of Celia in her light-colored blouse and short skirt, her shapely legs posed in the ridiculously high heels.

Something about spiked heels like that made a woman seem vulnerable, like she was almost hobbled, awaiting a man's pleasure. Alec shook his head, remembering how carefully and delicately Celia walked in the damn things.

He sure as hell hadn't been immune.

Then the door opened and closed again, voices spoke softly, and the young man was dismissed.

"Celia, it's good to see you again."

"Hello, Mr. Giles."

She sounded nervous, and Alec wanted to kick his own ass for not doing more to reassure her before letting her go. He'd been intent only on his own pleasures, and on keeping reality at bay. It was bad enough when he'd stupidly stayed the whole night with her, leaving their association open to discovery. Luckily, Jacobs felt she was safe and hadn't had her watched through the night. But it had still been pretty dark when Alec had left this morning, and he'd stuck to the shadows, being careful to avoid announcing his presence.

"What do you think of my studio?"

"It's...it's not quite what I expected."

"But it is perfect. The large space, the concrete floor and high ceilings, make setting up for shoots perfect. The reflection is ideal for my lighting equipment. I was thrilled to find it. And believe me, I've done some of my best work here."

"Then I'm really honored that you asked me to pose here."

"My pleasure." There was quiet, some shuffling. "Now, Celia, none of that. No blushes. There are few relationships as close as that between model and photographer, so you're going to have to accustom yourself to me touching you."

Touching her? Alec saw red and wanted to interrupt them right now. Much more of this stress and his heart would quit. Only Celia's soft, teasing voice calmed him.

"I'm just flustered to be here. I mean, it's so exciting! To think I might actually be in a magazine!"

"Oh, you'll definitely appear in the spread. I can almost guarantee that." There was a smile in the man's tone that set Alec's teeth on edge. "That is, if you allow me to do my job the best that I can—which means you're going to have to relax. Now, why don't we start with a few simple shots, and then you can change."

A small silence. "Change?"

"Of course." Alec heard a sound like a stool being dragged across the bare floor. "Here you go. Sit your pretty self right here in front of the backdrop while I adjust the lights."

"Oh. They're almost blinding. I can barely see."

"Don't worry about it, you'll get used to it. I can see perfectly, and that's what matters. Just put this leg here—that's right."

Celia giggled, making Alec want to punch through the brick wall he leaned against.

"And this leg like so—lovely. No, don't pull your knees together. This is to be a relaxed pose. Now, chin up and smile."

"Like this?"

"Come, Celia. You can do better than that." The

sound of a shutter clicking filled the air. "I want a coy, seductive look. Pretend you're waiting naked in bed for your lover."

She laughed, and the sound was strained. "But I don't have a lover."

Another pause. "Very nice—tilt your head." Then: "No lover? Why, that's an awful pity for a woman as sexy as yourself. Does this mean you're entirely free?"

"My eyes are watering."

"Go ahead and close them a minute." His voice was oily, calculating. "Can you answer me, please?"

"What? Oh, no, I'm totally free. I don't want to tie myself down with some possessive ape. There's too much I want to do still."

"Hmmm. Then perhaps you'd like to join me tonight for another party. You made quite an impression last night and there are a few other people Marc and I would like to introduce you to."

"Another party? My gosh, there's so much going on here!"

"Never a dull moment. So what do you say? Would you like to meet some more important people?"

Even before she spoke, Alec knew what she would say. The little idiot would disregard the order he'd given her.

"That would be wonderful!"

Alec plowed both hands through his hair. *Damn, damn, damn.*

"Excellent."

"Will there be anyone there I already know? Like Hannah and Jade?"

Alec groaned. *Don't push it, babe.* Though she merely sounded excited, he didn't want her taking any chances by trying to move too fast, or associating herself with one particular person.

"Oh, of course! Hannah is one of Marc's favorite girls. He takes her everywhere. I'm not sure about Jade, but I'll mention it to Marc. I'm sure he won't mind obliging you." There was the rustle of papers. "Here's the address. No, don't get up, I'll just stick it in your purse. Be there at six o'clock, dressed in something sexy. Actually, what you wore last night would work."

"Again? But—"

The paper crinkled against the transmitter, for the moment blocking out all other sounds. But luckily Giles didn't pay the pen any mind because Alec clearly heard the next words, telling him the pen hadn't been disturbed.

"You looked lovely in it, and no will notice or care, I promise you. Now, are you ready? Okay, turn the other way. No, like this."

"Oh!"

"You're very soft, Celia."

"Thank...thank you."

Alec's hands bunched into fists. Nothing that was happening could have been any worse than his imagination. He wanted to kill Giles with his bare hands.

"But it is hot under the lights, isn't it? Even the air-conditioning doesn't help. You must be smothering in that outfit."

Alec stiffened. The bastard. He was touching her and talking softly to her and he didn't even have the decency to try for a believable pretense! His line was so obvious, he may as well have said, *I want you naked now.*

Alec could feel Celia's hesitation when she nervously whispered, "It is rather warm."

"Well, lucky for you, the magazine ad calls for a lot of skin to show. Sometimes we're stuck modeling fur coats! That's really miserable, I can tell you. But the ad I have in mind for you is for an all-over body lotion. I have to send them several shots of different models so they can decide who best suits them, but I honestly believe you have the very best chance. All we need to do is convince them of that, and then you're on your way. Here you go, take this."

"What is it?"

A rough male laugh. "Your costume of sorts. You'll strip down and pose on the stool, using the length of velvet to insure your, ah, modesty. With your fair hair and golden eyes, along with the white backdrop, the red velvet will look...delicious, and make a startling contrast. You really do have excellent skin, so we need to show that off."

"I...ah..."

"Celia, you have a lovely body, one you should be proud of. Models are known, judged and selected for their bodies. If you're serious about this, you have to be willing to flaunt your assets. And believe me, your body, slim but with plenty of proper curves, is an asset. *Use it.*"

Say no, Alec thought, his mind rebelling, his muscles drawing tight, his heart crashing against his ribs, *refuse right now and get the hell out of there.*

There was a heavy pause, pregnant with anticipation, and then he heard Celia ask very softly, "Where should I change?"

Even as he was already moving, one plan after another jumping through his brain, Alec cursed and cursed again. When he got her home...

Thinking of a dire enough threat would slow him down, and right now he needed to keep his focus. He could, and would, figure out what to do with Celia later.

For now, he had to save her sweet little butt.

CELIA'S HEART DRUMMED so roughly she thought it might punch right through her chest. She clutched the red velvet in her fists, trying not to crush it, while fighting the urge to run.

This was her test. Giles was testing her, probably at Jacobs's urging, to see if she was genuine. A real model "wanna-be" in her desperate shoes would likely jump at the opportunity to show herself to favor, especially to the prestigious magazine people Giles claimed to know.

A real P.I. intent on saving another woman wouldn't hesitate to pass the damn test.

It didn't take her long to decide she had no choice, none at all. She would see Hannah tonight, and somehow she'd convince her. Maybe Jade, too. She'd like to shut Jacobs's entire operation down. She wanted him behind bars, where he couldn't ever hurt anyone again.

Her face turned red-hot as she thought about Alec listening in. It was even harder than she'd suspected, knowing he heard every word and that he was no doubt furious, cursing her even as she struggled with her decision. *Please understand, Alec. I have to do this, I have to save Hannah.*

Her train of thought stopped cold when Giles put his hand on her bottom, urging her behind a very slightly curtained area—thankfully still close to where her purse sat so that if need be, she could summon Alec.

"Hurry along now. We don't have all day. You can just leave your clothing—all of it—on the hooks on the wall."

Celia drew in a deep breath. The curtain wasn't all that wide or concealing. Giles could see her from the neck up and the knees down. Never had she felt so exposed, knowing he watched as she forced herself through such an uncomfortable, denigrating situation.

And that had to be his plan. She remembered Hannah telling her Giles enjoyed frightening women. She'd had a taste of his methods already while in Marc Jacobs's den, when Giles had pulled her close and kissed her. She'd wanted to throw up then, to claw his face. Holding back her panic had taken a lot of effort. But he'd known how the rapid familiarity had upset her, and he'd enjoyed it.

Remembering made Celia stiffen her spine. She wouldn't give the cretin the satisfaction of knowing how he'd thrown her off balance again.

Smiling at him, watching his face light up with interest and his green eyes darken, she laid the velvet over the curtain rod and began unbuttoning her blouse. "How long do you think it'll be before we hear about the photos?"

Giles rubbed his hands together, making Celia's stomach turn. His dark hair, usually immaculately in place, looked a little disheveled. Combined with the glee in his eyes, it gave him a slightly crazed look. "Not long, not long."

She kicked her shoes off, which safely lowered her breasts another three inches behind the concealment of the curtain. Her blouse was open now and she wondered if Giles could see the frantic racing of her heart, which caused a resultant trembling in her entire body. She shimmied her shoulders to remove the blouse completely, then put it on a hook. She let her bra straps slip down her arms. "I'm really anxious." She smiled again.

Giles stood, licking his lips and taking a step toward her—and suddenly alarms went off throughout the building. A loud, shrill series of horns and whistles blared and echoed everywhere, bouncing off the empty concrete walls.

Celia's eyes widened and she shouted, "What's going on?"

Giles, looking utterly panicked at the thought of an unknown threat, turned a complete, haphazard circle. He was obviously as confused as Celia by the alarm. And then the sprinkler system kicked in and water sprayed down on them both from high ceilings. Celia yelped, grabbing for her blouse and holding it over her head.

Giles cursed foully and leaped from his camera equipment to his elaborate lighting to his desk littered with papers, trying to cover everything at once, trying to shield things with his body. Celia looked around, uncertain what to do.

Giles spared her a frantic, harassed look. "Get the hell out of here before the fire department arrives!"

His shout was mean and within seconds other people were in the room, rushing to obey his barked orders. Celia hesitated only a moment more, then shoved her feet back in her shoes, snatched up her purse, and headed for the door she'd come through.

"Not that way!" Giles grabbed her naked arm, his grip bruising, and practically thrust her out through another exit. "Go down that corridor. There's a door that opens into the back parking lot. And get dressed for God's sake!"

Celia shoved wet hair out of her face and rushed to obey. Icy water continued to spray her. The pandemonium behind her dimmed as she trotted toward a blinking exit sign. But as she stepped outside, now grateful for the heat and blinding sunshine, curiosity got the better of her. This might be her only chance to spy a little. She looked back at the large brick structure, more a warehouse than a studio, and saw there was a row of dark windows on either side of the door she'd just come through.

She located a broken crate by a Dumpster and dragged it closer to the building. Her blouse was still clutched in her hand, her purse slung over her shoulder, her wet hair dripping down her back and making her shiver despite the warmth of the day.

Just as she started to step up on the crate, an iron-hard arm closed around her waist and jerked her down. She started to scream, but the sound was cut off by a callused palm flattening over her mouth. Her body came into contact with a solid chest, and then she heard a familiar whisper in her ear. "Not a sound, damn it. Someone's coming."

She was dragged behind the Dumpster and forced behind Alec's body while two slender male figures ran outside, soaked through to their skin, hauling camera equipment. When they went out of sight around the corner of the building, Alec pulled her up and grabbed her hand. "This way. And hurry."

She tried, she really did, but the shoes made haste nearly impossible. She started to kick them off, but Alec took her arm and kept her moving. Shoving her toward a retaining wall, he said, "Don't say a word. Not a single damn word."

Speaking was well beyond her anyway. She concentrated on discovering a way to scale the wall, when suddenly Alec grabbed her by the waist and practically threw her over it. Within a heartbeat he'd joined her and there was his truck on the side of the road, shielded by a cluster of wild bushes and a few sparse trees. They both jumped inside and Alec pulled away. "Keep your head down in case anyone sees us."

When she didn't react quickly enough, he flattened his large palm on the crown of her wet head and pushed her down in the seat, her cheek to his thigh. "Stay there until I tell you it's clear."

His idea of clear didn't come for some time. Her

head rested practically in his lap, her body twisted painfully. It was a good ten minutes before he stopped at a traffic light and looked down at her. He was plainly enraged.

With his foot tight on the brake, he skinned out of his cotton shirt and dropped it on her. "Put that on."

Celia narrowed her eyes. "Is it okay if I sit up now?"

A grudging, sharp nod was her only answer. Celia saw his hands flex on the steering wheel, his knuckles turning white. Cautiously, she slid up into the seat. For comfort's sake, she kicked out of her heels and dropped her sodden blouse onto the floor. Remembering his order to inform him of things up front, she said, "Ah, I have a party to go to tonight..."

"I heard."

He wouldn't look at her, and she felt bereft. Licking her lips, she tentatively asked, "The sprinkler system?"

"Always goes off when someone sets a fire."

"You?" She shouldn't have been so surprised. Alec was a quick thinker, and he obviously understood the predicament Giles had put her in. When he did no more than ignore her, she said, "Thank you."

And those soft, humble words seemed to set him off.

"*Goddammit, Celia.*" She jumped a good foot, then sat staring at him. He was beyond furious. "Do you have any idea at all what Giles would have done to you once he had you naked? I doubt screaming would have even brought you any aid, considering everyone on his payroll is likely dirty. You could have been—"

"I know."

"You know? *You know!*" He was so angry, she suspected his shouted words could be heard by the cars passing them by. His neck was red and his black eyes glowed like hot coals. "Then why in hell did you agree?"

"Because I had to. Because it was the test."

He put the truck in drive and lurched back into traffic. "And you have this harebrained idea that you owe the world something because of Raymond. You think you can make retribution? Baby, you don't know anything about it."

She drew in a slow breath. "It may have started out that way. At first, I only wanted to make myself feel better by helping other women. I did see it as a debt of sorts I had to pay." She reached across the seat and touched his arm, right where the tattoo decorated his biceps. She felt his muscle flinch. "But now, I *have* to do it. I have to save Hannah and the other girls—"

His head jerked around to stare at her. "*Other* girls?"

She drew a deep steadying breath. "I met Jade, a very young, very lovely girl, and there were others I didn't meet, but I saw them at the party. I don't doubt I'll see them again tonight." Her fingers tightened on his arm. "Alec, I want to shut Jacobs down."

Alec's fist hit the steering wheel. "*Goddammit!*"

She wished he'd quit swearing like that. It made her heart jump every time, and drove home how opposed he was to the entire effort. "He has to be stopped—"

"That's not what you're being paid to do." He tried to sound reasonable, but his voice shook. With anger? "Mrs. Barrington just wants Hannah back. The rest of it..."

"Yes?" She knew Alec's conscience, knew he wouldn't be able to abide the idea of Jacobs walking free any more than she could.

Surprised that the steering wheel didn't crack under his hands, Celia waited until finally Alec sighed. He flexed his jaw several times and she knew he was striving for control. "So do you have some grand plan that'll convict Jacobs without putting all the girls through the scandal, because believe me, the press will have a field day with a story like this. Every young woman involved will end up very well known for things they'd likely rather forget."

Lifting her chin, Celia said, "I'm going to be the one to testify against them. Blair Giles took pictures of me and made false promises—you heard that much."

"And have it on tape." His expression was stony, but resigned. "The receiver to your transmitter was attached to a small tape recorder."

Celia grinned at him, relieved that some of his anger seemed to be dissolving. "You're fantastic, Alec."

"You won't think so after I turn you over my knee for scaring me half to death."

Since Celia wasn't the least bit afraid of him or his ridiculous threat, she was able to keep her smile. "The thing is, I don't think the little bit we've gotten so far would be enough to convict Jacobs or Giles of anything. And I couldn't ask Hannah to testify. She's so afraid, and you're right, it would cause such a scandal and embarrass her so much." She scooted a little closer to Alec on the seat, then put her hand on his arm again. "I'm going to need to...*push,* just a little more tonight."

Alec swung the truck into the parking lot of his motel. Without a word, he got out and came around to her door. "Come on."

"I don't have much time..."

"You have enough time for me to shake some sense into you." Holding her arm in a firm grip, he led her toward his room.

Celia didn't even try to hold back. "Will you stop with the absurd threats, Alec. We both know you won't hurt me."

He gently pushed her inside and turned the dead bolt on the door. Arms crossed over his chest, he stood blocking the door, and gave her his most intimidating stare.

Celia shook her head. "That won't work, Alec. I'm not afraid of you anymore so you can just stop with the intimidation tactics."

He ignored her statement. "How exactly do you plan to push for more information?"

Celia licked her lips. Alec was in a very strange mood, and for the first time, she couldn't read him at all. "Well, of course I'll want to talk to Hannah again first, to see if I can convince her to leave with me. Then I'm going to act overly enthusiastic about Jacobs and Giles. I'm going to tell them I'll have to go home and give up on my dream if something doesn't happen, something that pays money. I'm going to be really desperate, and I'm going to let them know I'd be willing to do just about anything to gain fame."

Alec pushed away from the door. "No."

"Alec..."

"I've thought it over, and you're right. Jacobs and his cronies have to be stopped. But I'll do it, not you."

"You?"

"That's right." Alec paced, hands on hips, his expression thoughtful as he considered all his angles. "With you out of the picture, I won't be distracted. I can go back to Jacobs's, go through some things. Surely there's some incriminating information there, stored in his files or something. The more I've thought about it, the more certain I am that he'd have to keep information around to hold over the girls."

Celia glared at him as if he was insane. "You want to break into Jacobs's house? Alec, that's the dumbest damn thing you've ever said!" She grabbed his arm when he gave her an impatient look and continued to pace. Her hold stopped him. "Everything is already in place! What you're proposing would be far more dangerous and take a whole lot longer. I want Hannah out of there now, tonight if I can manage it."

Alec grabbed her, his hands tight around her upper arms, and he shook her. Shocked, Celia did no more than hang in his grip. He didn't hurt her, but he looked haunted as he leaned close and growled ferociously, "I don't want to see you hurt, damn it!" He shook her again, a revelation to Celia. "I *won't* see you hurt."

Celia slowly braced her hands against him. "Alec,

I'm a grown woman, responsible for myself." She searched his gaze, seeing so much for the first time. "If I choose to go there, if I choose to take a risk—a very minor risk, Alec—well, then, that's on me, not you. Do you understand me?"

He carefully lowered her feet back to the floor and released her. He took two steps back and he was breathing hard. "Of course I understand you. I'm not simple."

Celia watched him struggle for his famous control. She didn't know quite what else to say, but she knew now that if anything happened to her, he'd blame himself.

She couldn't let that happen. Big, strong, tough Alec had been hurt more than enough already. She wouldn't contribute to his wounds.

Rubbing the back of his neck with one hand, not looking at her, he said, "This could easily backfire on you."

"No. I'll be careful." She spoke softly, convincingly. "But either way, you're not responsible for the decisions I make."

He turned his back on her and that was all it took. Celia hugged him tight from behind. "Alec, I know you blame yourself for what happened to Marissa."

She felt his snort, as if in denial, but he said nothing.

"She was the same age as you, Alec, not a child you were supposed to take care of."

"She was my wife."

"And she was a mixed-up young lady who didn't know what she wanted or where to find it. She didn't ask you for help, and would have refused it in any case. You couldn't have done any more for her than you did."

"If I hadn't walked away from her that day—"

Celia interrupted with, "If I hadn't gotten involved with Raymond...?" She let the sentence dangle, showing him how useless it was to try to relive the past. "We're human and we make mistakes. Sometimes we're ruled by emotions, by our pride. Even the almighty Alec Sharpe has to deal with regret, but you can't let it change you forever."

He sighed, tipped his head back to stare at the ceiling. Celia could feel his frustration and indecision. She tightened her hold on him and kissed his shoulder. "I'm going tonight, Alec. And I know you'll be there, close if I need you. But if the impossible happens and things don't work out as I planned, then I won't have you blaming yourself. Now promise me."

He twisted around to face her, his gaze disturbingly intent, his expression enigmatic. "I'll promise you this. I'll be outside, watching and waiting. And if I hear so much as a peep that alarms me, if I see one shadow that worries me, or I have one mistrustful intuition, I'm ending it."

Celia supposed that was the best she could get from a man like Alec. He'd worry until it was over, and there was nothing she could do about it. She'd just have to be extra careful to survive unscathed, to prove she could and would handle herself with intelligence and discretion.

She stared back at him and nodded. "All right, Alec."

He tipped up her chin. "And lady, when this is over, it's over. Everything. Because I can't take it anymore."

Including their relationship? She didn't want to, but again she agreed with a small nod. Then, before she had a chance to get emotional again, she went to his phone to call a cab. She only had a few hours left before she needed to be at the party. Alec couldn't take the risk of driving her back to her hotel, not when there was the possibility he might be seen.

Evidently he wouldn't take the risk of caring for her either. After tonight, she'd have met her goals of saving Hannah Barrington. But with her unwavering determination, she'd driven Alec nuts, and lost out on any hope of having his love.

It was hard to feel happy over her success, when she'd just lost everything she'd ever really wanted.

12

"HANNAH, I'D LIKE to talk to you."

Hannah barely spared her a glance. "No, leave me alone."

Celia caught her arm as the girl started to stride away. It was the very first chance Celia had of speaking with her. Jacobs and Giles had at first loomed at Celia's side continually, introducing her to several gentlemen and only a few ladies. Giles had tried to laugh off the incident at the warehouse, but his tension was plain to see, and the damage was still being assessed. He apologized gallantly to Celia for his rough treatment of her, explaining that his equipment meant the world to him—without it, he couldn't serve lovely women like herself. Celia had almost snorted at that inane apology.

She had no idea how Alec had started the fire, or what he'd burned. But she could tell by the stilted conversation in both Giles and Jacobs, the incident had put them both on edge. They seemed more alert, more cautious.

Then a waiter had come to whisper to Jacobs and he'd gone to take care of some business. Celia didn't care what the business was as long as Giles went with him.

He didn't, but he did dismiss himself a few

minutes later with the promise he'd return to her quickly. Hannah had steered clear of them all, hovering around the wet bar set up in a far corner, grinning and laughing, but Celia saw new circles under her eyes, and a wariness that went bone-deep.

"If you avoid me like this, it'll cause suspicion."

Hannah's gaze widened. Then with a furtive look around, she allowed Celia to tug her over to a small settee situated in a corner of the room. Celia could see all the entrances, everyone coming and going, and there was no way anyone could sneak up on her or overhear her conversations with Hannah.

"Talk to me, Hannah. Please."

Hannah closed her eyes and swallowed hard. Chandelier lights glinted in her gold-and-diamond earrings and reflected off the colorful sequins of her skimpy gown. If Celia hadn't been so intent on other matters, she'd have felt like a total frump in the same black pantsuit. In an effort to at least give the illusion of a different outfit, she'd added a colorful red, lemon and black scarf to her hair, and brightly colored earrings that matched. She figured any woman out to attract the attention of producers would make the effort to present her best appearance. Giles had approved.

"There's nothing to talk about, Celia. I can't go home."

"Can't, or won't?"

"Both. Please, understand. You're wasting your time."

"Your mother doesn't think so, Hannah. Your whole family is devastated that they haven't heard from you, that you're avoiding them. Your mother even thinks you've been brainwashed." Celia smiled sadly. "Or that you're being blackmailed."

An almost desperate laugh escaped Hannah. "My mother was always overdramatizing things."

Celia took her hand and held it. The girl's fingers were cold and stiff. Very gently, Celia asked, "Is she dramatizing now, Hannah?"

Hannah bit her lip and large tears gathered in her eyes. She stared at her lap, at first not answering. Then with a tiny shake of her head, she whispered, "No."

"Ah." Celia felt elated over the small concession, elated and frantic to find out all she could while Hannah was willing to talk. "How is Jacobs keeping you here?"

Hannah turned to look at her. "I've been so stupid." Her smile was filled with self-loathing. "At first, Marc seemed so nice. He helped me out, got me a few photo shoots. I never saw the ads, but I did get the money. He advanced it to me for an apartment, for the new clothes I needed to compete for other photo opportunities. But then, all of a sudden I owed him back more than I could make. The apartment is extravagant, but I signed a lease because Jacobs told me I could eventually afford it. It's owned by another friend of his."

Celia could easily see the circle growing, could envision how a woman would be trapped in Jacobs's web of friends.

"He...he offered me new ways to make more money. And I...I thought it was just a paid escort service." She stared at Celia, desperate. "That's what he told me it was."

Hannah covered her mouth and struggled to keep from crying. Celia quickly patted her back, murmuring to her. "It's all right. I understand. Take a few deep breaths. You have to get control, Hannah. If Jacobs or Giles sees you crying, they'll wonder what we're talking about. Either of them could come back any minute."

"I'm sorry." She groped for the tissue Celia handed to her and dabbed at her eyes. "I almost never cry anymore. There's no point to it. But things just went so wrong so fast—"

"I know." Still trying to soothe Hannah with a gentle pat to her shoulder, Celia asked, "The escort service was a ruse?"

Again Hannah nodded. "I met a man, and we...I thought we hit it off. He was kind and gentle, and he seemed so sincere. I was so lonely then, and scared and everything was confused." She bit her lip and her cheeks warmed. "We slept together that very first night. He told me I was beautiful and that he couldn't stop wanting to touch me. For the first time in months, things felt right."

Keeping a careful watch out for Jacobs or Giles, and at the same time smiling at the milling crowd so no one would suspect them, Celia asked, "But it wasn't?"

Dully, as if she hardly cared anymore, Hannah said, "When I woke up the next morning, he was gone and there was money beside my bed. He'd...he'd paid me. Like a prostitute." She drew a deep breath and continued. "I was embarrassed and hurt, and I wanted to give the money back to him, but I didn't know where he lived or what his phone number was. Marc just laughed at me when I told him about it, saying I didn't have any reason to be upset, that this would be the perfect way for me to offset my costs and to begin paying him back. I wanted to just walk away. I thought my mother would welcome me back, even though I'd been so awful when I left. But that's when he told me about the photos he had." She looked at Celia, her face filled with desperation. "My family would be so embarrassed, and it'd be all my fault."

Celia felt herself shaking from head to toe. Her suspicions had been correct, but still she was shocked. *Prostitution.* And blackmail. A deep rage filled her when she thought of Jacobs ruthlessly plotting against such a sweet young woman. Celia griped Hannah's hand. "He's an animal, a bastard. But we can take care of that now, Hannah."

"No. My mother would die if those pictures were made public. I thought they were for legitimate magazine ads, but Blair knows how to doctor them so they look even worse than they really did. He showed me a couple, and they were so...so ugly. No, I could never do that to my family."

Celia reached into her purse and withdrew a slip of paper. On it, she wrote the number Alec had made her memorize, the one that reached his cell phone. She stuffed it into Hannah's hand. "I'm going to try to end all this tonight, Hannah. With any luck, Jacobs and Giles will both be going to jail, along with anyone else who works with them. But if you get into any trouble, if you need help at all, I want you to call that number. I promise if you do, everything will be all right."

Hannah looked up, and her wide-eyed expression caused Celia to do the same. She saw both Jacobs and Giles headed toward them and she stood to greet them, smiling as she saw Hannah stuff the small slip of paper into the top of her dress, between her breasts.

"I wondered where you'd both gotten to! I wanted to go looking for you, but Hannah told me we should just wait. She's been very nice in keeping me entertained."

Jacobs smiled at Hannah and pulled her close, his hand resting possessively on her hip. "Well, I have a treat for you, Celia."

With a suitably anxious look, Celia asked, "A treat?"

Giles rubbed his hands. "We're going to go meet a producer. I showed him some of your photos and he's very impressed. He wants to meet you tonight."

"Now?" Celia's mind squirrelled around for some way to postpone the meeting, knowing Alec would be outraged. She caught a glimpse of Hannah, who looked appalled by the change in plans, which confirmed in Celia's mind that the threat now was real. But then Giles took her hand and started to lead her away.

"Come, I'll tell you all about it. But we have to hurry."

She glanced back at her purse on the settee, where

the pen transmitter was. Unfortunately, when she'd stood, the cushion moved and the purse had dumped. "Oh no, my purse."

Jacobs looked down, scooped up several things and stuffed them back inside. "Here you go. Now hurry along."

Celia, still being tugged along by Giles, saw that the pen was missing. "Wait! My pen—"

"I have plenty of pens, Celia. Don't give it another thought."

"But...it has sentimental value to me."

"I'll call Marc later and have him look for it."

"But..."

"Celia, we need to go. Don't worry. Marc and Hannah will be joining us."

She had no idea how to argue beyond that. With one last wistful look at the settee, she gave up and forced a smile for Giles. There really wasn't anything else she could do. Trying to sound enthusiastic, she asked, "A producer you say?" but in her mind, she was thinking that getting through this new meeting would likely be a piece of cake, compared to how Alec would react when he caught up to her.

"ARE YOU SURE we're at the right place?" No matter how she tried, Celia couldn't begin to look relaxed. The luxurious resort cabin Blair Giles took her to was remote and it didn't appear to have had a single soul in residence for some time. At least, not a permanent resident. The cottage seemed more like a carefully selected site for doing business. The kind of business is what bothered Celia.

While Giles made himself at home, turning on a minimum of lights and mixing drinks at the small bar, she looked around. The cathedral ceiling was tinted glass, allowing the many stars and muted moonlight to shine through. She could just see the edges of a few branches from tall trees brushing over the roof. The air was heavy with silence, broken only by the clink of ice being dropped into glasses.

"Relax, Celia. He'll be here. Later."

She gulped hard, trying to find a drop of spit in her very dry mouth. "Later?"

Giles grinned widely at her and his eyes were lit like green fire. For the first time, she noticed that he had a gold tooth toward the back of his mouth. She crossed her arms over her bare midriff as he approached.

"Here, drink this. It'll help to calm you."

There was no way she was putting a single sip of alcohol into her system. She needed to be totally clearheaded to deal with this new situation. After setting the glass aside—which made Giles frown—she said, "Blair, I thought we were meeting some other people here. I had no idea you were planning this...this..." She gestured with her hand, indicating the intimate and isolated atmosphere of the cottage.

"This romantic setting?" he supplied, one brow raised, his voice smooth and seductive. "I'm sorry, Celia, but I was desperate to get you alone. And I promise you, you'll meet all the producers you could possibly need. I can already see what a success you're going to be."

He stepped closer and Celia stepped back. She was

very afraid. "You mean, you made this up?" While she spoke, she looked around, trying to find some avenue of escape. Not a single hope presented itself. The furniture all looked heavy and masculine. A few statuettes were placed in the corners, and there were heavy ceramic ashtrays on the tables, along with tall deco lamps and a few books.

They were on the ground floor, and a loft was overhead, but there didn't appear to be any exits from there, just the bedroom.

She glanced back to see Giles watching her closely, his expression expectant. He wanted her to try something, she realized. He wanted her afraid and running, so he could chase her down. Instead, she looked directly at him, waiting for an answer.

His smile wavered slightly. "No, of course not. But our guests will come later. Much later."

When the back of her knees hit the sofa, her eyes widened. "Later? But it's almost midnight already."

"Did you have other plans?" He slowly, carefully, took her hands in his, as if savoring the moment.

Celia remembered how this particular man reacted to a woman's fear. By backing away from him, she'd added to his enjoyment of the moment. No more; she wouldn't give him what he wanted, either physically or emotionally.

What would Alec do now? How would he react if he were here?

Trying to clear her mind, Celia forced a smile and abruptly sat down, curling close in the corner of the sofa. She stretched her arms out, at her leisure. The fingertips of her left hand touched the edge of the heavy ashtray, but she couldn't get a good grip on it without being obvious.

Trying to look coy and stall for time, she said, "You really went to all this trouble just for me?"

Eyes narrowed, Giles suddenly reached down and jerked her to her feet. As if impassioned, he pulled her close and said against her mouth, "I want you so damn bad, I'd do just about anything to see it happen." She twisted and his mouth landed on her cheek. "Believe me, I don't usually react this way with the models. But you're different, so lovely and innocent..."

"No!"

One of his hands held the back of her neck with painful force, keeping her from turning her face away from his mouth, while the other clutched at her bottom. He wasn't much taller than her and when he yanked her close, her body came into vivid contact with his from knees to breasts. Her stomach jolted sickly, her skin crawled.

Celia cried out. Reacting solely on instinct, her intentions flown with her panic, she fought him. Though he might look soft and ineffectual, he was a man with a man's strength. He laughed, and when his mouth touched hers again, she bit him.

Giles became giddy, delighted with her fight. "Marc told me I should wait, that I shouldn't rush you. But I knew he was wrong, I knew you'd be perfect."

His hand knotted in her hair and pulled her head back so he could stare down at her breasts. Her scalp burned, but worse than that, she felt his mouth, wet and hot, on her flesh and she simply couldn't stand it.

Allowing her knees to buckle, she dropped, giving him all her weight and losing a lot of hair in the process. He stumbled, trying to hold onto her, but they both fell to the carpet. Celia immediately scrambled back, Giles grabbing for her kicking legs, and when she reached for the table and felt the ashtray, she didn't hesitate. She swung it hard at his head. Giles chuckled, ducking, but the idiot wasn't fast enough. Her next swing hit him in the side of the head with a sickening thunk. He stared blankly at her for only a moment, then his eyes rolled back and he slumped to the carpet.

Celia scrambled to her feet. The crop top to her pantsuit was torn, one shoulder seam hanging so low her nipple was barely covered. Trembling from head to toe, she tried to pull it up, but it kept falling back. She heaved, trying to breathe, trying to get her mind to settle so she could think. All she wanted was to run away, but she wouldn't get far on foot and she didn't know if he'd wake soon and come after her.

She thought about hitting him again, but couldn't bring herself to bludgeon him while he was already unconscious. Swallowing back the tears that would do her no good, she flexed her shoulders, trying to think.

Keys. She'd take his keys and drive away. Not wanting to, but seeing no help for it, she dropped to her knees beside Giles and tried to decide which pocket he'd put the keys in. She was just reaching for him when the door opened and she gave a startled scream, her wild gaze flying up to see who had entered.

Jacobs stood there, his long-fingered hand wrapped tight around Hannah's arm. His gaze moved from Celia, her hair tossed, her makeup ruined, her clothes torn, to Giles out cold on the floor, his temple swollen and spotted with blood. He shook his head in disgust. "I told that damn idiot to wait, but he wouldn't listen."

The door slammed behind him and he roughly shoved Hannah into the room. The girl tripped and almost fell but Celia caught her, helping her to regain her balance. Very slowly, she faced Jacobs, stepping in front of Hannah.

"What are you doing here?"

With two fingers, Jacobs help up the piece of paper she'd given to Hannah. "Conspiring against me, weren't you?"

The bottom dropped out of her stomach. "Hannah had nothing to do with that. I just wanted—"

"Sit down and shut up." Jacobs pulled a gun from inside his suitcoat and waved it at the two women. Trying to stay calm, Celia took Hannah's hand and led her to the sofa. The poor girl was trembling all over, her face totally leeched of color.

"I'm sorry," she whispered to Celia, shaking her head. "I knew what was happening and I wanted to help you. I didn't mean for him to find out..."

"Shhh. I know. It's all right."

Jacobs nudged Giles with his foot, and was rewarded with a moan. "Get up you ass or I'll shoot you to save myself the bother of dealing with your idiocy."

Giles moaned again and very gingerly pulled himself into a sitting position. His hand touched his head, and then recognition came. "The little bitch hit me!"

"She did better than that. She knocked you out cold." Jacobs smirked. "Doesn't say much for your seductive powers, now does it?"

Giles roared to his feet, his face bright red with both pain and humiliation. As he lurched toward Celia, sure death in his eyes, she pressed herself back on the sofa. But Jacobs brought him up short with a fist knotted in his collar. "No, don't touch her yet. There's something you need to know."

Giles, heaving in his anger, turned to stare at Jacobs. "Well?"

"Your warehouse caught fire again."

"What!"

"I don't know all the details yet. But evidently whoever set that little fire at the studio returned." Jacobs grinned at Giles' horrified expression and then flicked a glance at Celia. "It's lucky for you, Blair, that I keep my own files because you've had a total loss."

Stammering in his grief, Giles asked, "My photos...?"

"Gone. Every one of them." Jacobs waved at Celia with the gun. "I think we should ask our newest guest here about that. It seems a real coincidence that all the trouble started when she got involved. Well, Celia? Do you want to talk to me or should I let Giles go ahead and have his fun with your body first?"

Celia lifted her chin; bravado was all she had left

and she'd use it for Hannah's sake as well as her own. "Touch me and you'll regret it. I'm not afraid of you, of either of you. And if you don't let us go right now, I'll testify against you both and you'll spend the rest of your lives in jail."

Jacobs thought her threat was immeasurably funny, judging by his loud laugh. Giles did little more than glare at her. "Did you hear her, Blair? She's going to testify against us."

Giles slanted her an evil look. "Give me a few hours with her before you kill her."

Hannah began to cry softly, but Celia ignored her for the moment. They meant to intimidate her, to break her. But she'd been dealing with Alec for too long to shrivel up and fall apart over a few threatening words. She gave them both a look of contempt, the best she could muster, then said, "You're both too damn stupid to realize it's all over. Do you really think I'd have come here alone? A woman, by myself?"

Jacobs snarled a curse and retaliated against her contempt by backhanding her. Since Jacobs had gone from confident good humor to outright rage in an instant, Celia hadn't been at all prepared for the blow. Even when she saw it coming, she didn't have time to do more than gasp before she was knocked completely off the sofa. Crying out, she landed hard on the floor, bruising her knees and scraping her palms. Her head felt as if it had exploded and she prayed she wasn't wrong about Alec, that he'd somehow, despite the fact she'd lost her wired pen, known where she was going, that he wasn't far behind.

As if she'd summoned him with her desperation, Alec chose that exact moment to burst through the door. He literally kicked it in, causing wood to splinter and glass to crack, and Celia, thankful that he was on her side, wondered how one man could manage so much menace by his mere presence. He looked like an enraged bull, his dark eyes filled with murder. When his gaze quickly took in the entire scene and he saw Celia on her knees, holding her cheek, he gave a shout of rage reminiscent of a berserker that made all the windows rattle.

Hannah crouched down beside Celia, clutching at her and hiding her face in her shoulder. Giles completely froze, his face paper-white with terror and his hands up as if to ward off evil.

That left Jacobs, and he tried to bring the gun up and around in time, but Alec was already on him. His first kick sent the gun clattering across the room to crash against the stone fireplace. His second kick had Jacobs grabbing his ribs, shouting in pain.

Celia was still a little stunned, watching the whole thing in fascinated horror, her heart fluttering, her body frozen. She seemed to see it in slow motion, but in truth, Alec's movements were a blur. From the time he'd burst in to putting Jacobs on the floor had taken little more than a few seconds. She felt awed by seeing Alec in action, though she'd heard enough stories she shouldn't have been surprised.

Despite her fascination, she noticed when Giles suddenly moved, trying to run across the room after the gun, and she reacted quickly. Shoving Hannah aside, she told the girl, "Get back," then leaped after

Giles. The man was just about to bend over for the gun when Celia threw herself on his back. Her weight knocked him off balance and the momentum of his reach kept him going headfirst into the stone fireplace. Once again, he slumped down unconscious and Celia gave only a brief thought as to whether or not she'd killed him this time.

Through the broken front door she heard the distant approach of sirens. She grabbed for the fireplace poker to help Alec, but when she turned, she saw that Jacobs wasn't fighting anymore. He merely dangled in Alec's grip, taking the punishment Alec seemed intent on doling out. Marc Jacobs's face was no longer handsome, but grotesquely swollen, and his fair hair was matted with blood.

Celia, filled with a new horror, threw the poker aside and leaped onto Alec's back this time. "Alec, no!"

Neither her weight nor her shout seemed to have any impact on him. He drew back to hit Jacobs again and Celia yelled right into his ear, "I love you, Alec!"

He froze with his fist in midair. Jacobs hung limply in his grip, making mewling sounds, and Alec released him to fall with a loud thump to the floor. Celia scrambled around to face Alec, desperate to reach him. "If you kill him, you'll end up in jail."

Alec didn't say anything, just stared at her. His face was still set, his eyes hard and distant, as if he had trouble bringing himself back under control. His chest moved slowly as he drew deep breaths.

Celia's heart began to beat so hard it hurt. She couldn't believe what she'd told him, but at least it had gotten him to stop. "Do...do you remember when I wanted to kill Raymond, and you told me it would only complicate my life?"

Still Alec stared at her. "I remember."

She dropped her gaze to his chest, touched his collarbone. "I don't want your life complicated because of me, Alec."

His fingers gently brushed her bruised, swollen cheek. His voice was low and full of concern when he asked, "Are you all right?"

"Other than a headache, I'm fine." Then she glanced at Giles. "I imagine his head hurts much worse." She couldn't help herself, she grinned nervously. "I knocked him out twice."

Alec didn't smile. Instead he walked toward the fireplace, continually looking back at Celia with a narrow-eyed gaze, as if afraid to let her out of his sight. He picked up the gun by the end of the barrel and set it out of reach. The sirens grew steadily louder.

Celia turned to find Hannah, pressed up to a wall, her eyes wide on Alec. Celia grinned. She remembered having that exact same reaction the first time she'd met Alec Sharpe. No man had ever affected her, frightened her, touched her, the way he had. He could scare the breath out of grown men with a look, but he was the gentlest, most honorable man she knew. "Hannah, this is a good friend of mine, Alec Sharpe. He's been working with me to help get you away from Jacobs."

Alec nodded to the girl, who blinked cautiously.

"Come here, Hannah. He won't bite."

Alec gave her a heated look, reminding her that he did in fact indulge in a nibble every now and again. Celia felt a blush start and wanted to smack him. "Alec, quit intimidating her."

With a wry frown at Celia, Alec removed his cotton shirt and gently slipped it over Hannah's shoulders. "She's in shock. See if you can find her something sweet to drink and a cold rag. I'll take care of these two." Alec started to turn away, then suddenly stopped. "Oh, Hannah? Any evidence they had against you is gone."

Hannah stared from Alec to Celia and back again. She gave a very fainthearted, "Oh?"

Alec nodded. "The inside of the warehouse was gutted, the files all caught on fire."

Celia nearly burst with pride. She just knew Alec was responsible for that. "When did that happen, Alec?"

"While you were getting ready for your damn party."

She grinned again.

With a completely straight face, he added to Hannah, "And I just found out that someone broke into Marc Jacobs's house and emptied out his office. No fire there, just a burglary it seems. There's enough evidence left to convict him, but nothing that will embarrass you in any way."

Unable to hold back a moment more, Celia released Hannah to throw her arms around Alec's neck. He gathered her close in a breath-depriving bear hug, lifting her completely off her feet and pressing his face hard into her neck.

"You're wonderful, Alec," she managed to squeak when his hold loosened.

To her surprise, he suddenly set her away from him and said, "Go wait in the kitchenette with Hannah. I'll take care of the cops and then we'll talk later." There was so much coldness in him, she flinched.

"Alec?"

His expression darkened and his jaw worked. He bent low, jutting out his chin and looking her in the eye. In guttural tones, he said, "You almost died." Glancing at Hannah, he said, "And her, too. Do you have any idea what would have happened if Hannah hadn't called me? If I hadn't gotten here when I did?"

Celia took a step back, and she too, glanced at Hannah. The girl gave her a weak, apologetic shrug. "She called you?"

"Thank God you at least had the sense to give her my number before you ran off with a lunatic, *without* the wire."

Celia shifted. "The pen fell into the couch and I couldn't—"

"Save it for later." Alec cut her off, apparently not interested in her excuses. "I'll take care of everything from here on. Hopefully I can manage better than **you** did."

He turned away to greet several uniformed officers who came cautiously through the door, guns drawn. Celia wanted to grab him, to pull him back, to explain. She felt a chill creeping up on her and realized the night air had cooled considerably, but her chill was more from the inside out. Still, she rubbed her hands up and down her bare arms.

Then she turned to see Hannah standing there shivering, wrapped in Alec's flannel. Her eyes were dilated, her cheeks pale. As he'd said, she easily could have been killed and it would have been her fault. Celia had no idea what Jacobs had done to her after finding the slip of paper on her. They both might have died if it hadn't been for Alec.

Celia looked around as cops stepped through the room. One of them glanced at her torn outfit and, blushing, handed her his jacket. Celia accepted it gratefully, suddenly anxious to cover herself, to hide the evidence of what she'd just gone through.

The house was in a shambles with a shattered door and broken furniture. Two men were unconscious on the floor, blood seeping into the beautiful carpet. She didn't even know who owned the cottage.

For a minute there, she'd been on an adrenaline high, pleased with the fact she'd survived, that Jacobs's madness was at an end. But Alec's censure had cut through all that.

She closed her eyes. Oh God, she'd made a mess of things. Alec had told her, had warned her. And now he was angry. But there was no way he could be more disappointed than she was.

Alec was right. She wasn't cut out for this. And as he'd said, it was all at an end.

She'd been a fool.

ALEC WATCHED CELIA walk numbly through the motel room. It was nearly dawn and he knew she was beat, but as usual, she held herself together without complaining. He wished she'd talk to him, give her usual chatter. She hadn't voluntarily said two words to him since the police had finished their questioning. By the time they were through, Alec figured he'd met damn near every officer in the unit. Jacobs had been transferred to a hospital, though Alec knew the bastard was all right.

Thanks to Celia.

If she hadn't stopped him, he very well might have done serious damage. He didn't want to think he was capable of actually killing so easily, but when he'd seen Jacobs hit her through the door window, when he crashed in and saw Celia down on the floor, her face bruised, he'd lost all reason. Never in his life had he been in such a killing rage. Yet Celia had stopped him with three little words. *I love you.*

Alec cocked a brow. At the moment, she didn't look too fond of him. She looked dejected and hurt and it damn near brought him to his knees. He knew he *would* kill for her. Hell, he'd die for her if it ever came to that. She meant so much to him he was still shaking from the near miss of maybe losing her. His hurtful words, and he knew damn well they had been hurtful, had been more a gut reaction to his own fear than anything else.

Crossing his arms over his chest, he leaned against the wall and watched her open her suitcase onto the bed. She began stuffing clothes inside, moving by rote, with no real thought involved. Alec sighed. "Hannah seemed anxious to get home to her mother."

He got his first smile in hours, and it didn't even rate as a full-fledged sign of cheer, more like weary relief. "Once she knew Jacobs and Giles couldn't embarrass her family with any photos she was agreeable. Especially when I told her all the lengths her mother had gone to just to get her back."

"They really won't be ashamed will they? Because her involvement will come out in the trial. People will know what happened, they just won't have pictures to go with the story."

Her smile this time was more genuine, if a little sad. "I knew you were responsible for that. All that nonsense about a break-in—"

"Was my way of covering my ass. I figured while you prettied up for your party, I should make good use of my time. I kept my cell phone close so you could reach me if you'd needed to."

"The chances you took going there..."

Alec shrugged. He was never the one at risk, but he didn't say so just yet. "I didn't destroy the whole warehouse, just the stuff that might embarrass the girls. The same is true of Jacobs's files. I slipped in there easily enough and within minutes found everything I was looking for. It never ceases to amaze me the evidence some people keep around, arrogantly thinking they'll never be caught. There's plenty there to prove what a scum he is, just nothing that will make innocent people pay."

Celia sighed. "You're pretty wonderful, Alec, you know that?"

His heart tripped and his muscles tightened. "Is that why you're trying to run away from me again?"

Her hands full of clothes, Celia looked up in surprise. "I'm not."

He pointed out the obvious. "You're packing."

She looked confused, then finally shook her head. "It's time to go home. We're done here. You said so yourself."

Alec narrowed his eyes and said low, "We had a deal, lady."

She dropped the clothes and stared up at him. "You're kidding, right?"

Very slowly he shook his head, then advanced on her. If he didn't touch her soon he was going to lose it. When he was standing right in front of her, he said, "You promised to do what I want if I helped, and the day isn't over yet. I figure you still owe me till morning."

"Alec..."

"I want you in bed." He scooped up her suitcase and dropped it on the floor. Clothes fluttered out, and he gained Celia's immediate ire. She went on tiptoe to yell at him, making it damn near impossible for him to hold back a smile. He'd take her fire any day over the dejection she'd just been feeling.

With one finger, she pointed at the bed while never looking away from him. "That is the very *worst* place for me. Yes, I made a deal with you, but that was when..." Her voice trailed off. She dropped back flat on her feet and stepped away. She bit her bottom lip.

Alec picked her up and, despite her struggles, got her stretched out on her back on the mattress. "When what, honey?" He kissed her beautiful face, her tipped-up nose, her lush mouth. "Tell me."

Celia turned her face away. "When I thought I could stand it. When I thought I could love you and just walk away."

His heart breaking, Alec touched her chin and brought her gaze back around to his. Celia drew in a deep breath. "But I'm not as strong as you, Alec. And Jacobs's little slap didn't hurt nearly as much as your rejection and lack of respect."

"Celia." He'd held back too long, and kissing her seemed like the most important thing in the world to him, an affirmation that she was truly alive and well.

Celia didn't fight him. Her mouth opened to his, and the kiss was gentle but deep, hungry and giving. Alec cupped her face in his hands, careful not to hurt her bruised cheek, and fed off her, knowing he'd never have enough, that three lifetimes wouldn't be enough with this woman.

When he finally pulled back she gulped down a sob and practically yelled right in his face, "You're a fool, Alec Sharpe! And a damned coward." Her voice cracked and she said in a quavering tones, "Because if you weren't, you wouldn't give up on love."

Alec smiled. "I know."

"You're also—what do you mean, you know?"

It was past time he told her how he felt, how much she meant to him. "I respect you, Celia. More than any man or woman I know. You believe in something, like saving Hannah, then you do whatever it takes to get the job done. Not many people have that much conviction, or are that brave."

"Really?"

She looked so skeptical he wanted to bundle her up

close and never let anything hurt her again. "I also trust you, and worry about you." He kissed her, a kiss so giving he had to fight his own tears. "And I love you. More than anything this earth has to offer."

She sucked in a startled breath. "You love me?"

Alec swallowed hard, then scowled, trying to cover his loss of control. "Hell, I must, otherwise I surely would have strangled you by now for always scaring me half to death. Look at what you do to me, honey."

He held out his hand and they both saw that he was still shaking like a wet pup. His voice dropped even lower and he groaned, "I thought I might lose you, and that's something I couldn't bear. You're right when you say I'm a coward. I used to be afraid of what you made me feel, of how you affected me. Now I'm just afraid of having to go on without you."

Big tears slid down her cheeks, but they were happy tears. "Oh, Alec, I was so scared!"

He understood the delayed reaction, of how the adrenaline rush would wear off and you were left depleted and hollow inside. He settled his body more firmly over hers, surrounding her with himself, his heat and his love. He whispered, "The fear is normal, babe. But the important thing is that you kept your head. You didn't panic and you reacted when you needed to. Everyone gets in over his head every now and then, and you're not immune. But you handled yourself well, and I think you've more than proved you have what it takes to make a great P.I."

His very well-rehearsed speech was met with mute surprise.

Alec cleared his throat. "I'd only ask two things,

though. One, that you not endanger yourself like that again. No more undercover stuff because my heart really can't take it. And two—"

Celia laid her palm on his mouth. She was smiling, a wide, happy smile now. "Alec, when I said I was afraid, I wasn't talking about today, though that was pretty scary, too. I meant I was so afraid that you'd never want me, that you'd never love me back."

He kissed her palm and then pulled her hand away. "Not a chance, babe. You're definitely stuck with me."

"Alec." All the love she felt was there for him to see, and now, it filled him up rather than shaking him.

He wanted to get back to business and see things settled. "Number two, would you marry me, Celia?"

She froze for a heartbeat, then squealed in excitement. Alec laughed, aware of how tense he'd been holding himself, not sure of her answer because he'd never been easy with her. But with the choke hold she had on his neck, he figured her answer was yes. He still wanted to hear her say it.

"Answer me, woman."

"Yes!"

"And about the undercover work?"

Celia pulled back just enough to laugh in his face. "Alec Sharpe, being married to you will likely be all the excitement I need."

As she pulled his head back down, intent on seducing him if he didn't miss his guess, Alec muttered, "Somehow I don't think I'll be able to hold you to that..."

Epilogue

"YOU KNOW EVERYONE'S going to think you're pregnant with the way Alec rushed things."

Celia looked down at where Angel, moderately pregnant herself, straightened a ruffle in Celia's elegant wedding gown. Alec had somehow, with her mother's help, gotten everything arranged in just under two months.

"My mother is hopeful." Celia grinned, knowing that didn't quite answer Angel's implied question. But she had no intention of telling anyone until after she'd told the father.

Angel scowled and slowly straightened. Dane, Angel's overly doting husband, came into the room just then and hurried to assist his wife.

"You shouldn't be bending like that," he said, and gently hauled her to her feet. Once there, he pulled her close and kissed her—then didn't want to stop kissing her. Celia just smiled, since Alec now behaved in a similar fashion, always touching her, kissing her, making sinfully naughty, exciting promises in her ear that he knew would make her blush and make everyone else curious.

She blushed now, just thinking of the night to come. *Her wedding night.*

Angel pulled away, then shook her head at both Dane and Celia. "You two are incorrigible. Just look at you both. Dane, behave. And Celia, what in the world are you blushing about? It's not like you shouldn't be used to your brother by now."

Dane chuckled. "She's used to me. It's Alec that has her getting all flustered. You should see him pacing around outside. If I didn't know better, I'd swear he was actually nervous. And he asked me how long he had to hang out at the reception before he and Celia could get away. Good grief, you'd think he could at least wait a few hours." Dane cast a teasing glance at his sister. "I think you've managed to pickle his brain."

Angel sniffed. "If you'll recall, I said all along they were meant for each other."

"Yes, you did. But it still boggles the mind." He cast another swift glance at Celia. "I thought she drove him crazy. And he's such a damn loner—"

Celia sighed. "*Used* to be a loner—not anymore. And for your information, I do drive him crazy. It's one of my more redeeming qualities. He says it keeps him on his toes."

Dane and Angel both grinned. "Is *that* what it does to him?"

Organ music started in the background. Celia had been in the room for over an hour, getting the last-minute primping taken care of, with Angel's help. She should have known her brother wouldn't be able to stay away from his wife that long.

She started to shoo them out the door so they could take their places, when suddenly Alec was there, looming in the doorway, looking incredibly sexy in his black tux. His golden earring glinted, but his hair had been trimmed, still a little long, but there was no need to tie it back. Celia sort of missed that ponytail, but even without it, he was gorgeous enough to bring the heat right back to her face.

He looked vastly annoyed and gave her his patented killer glare, which still made grown men cower but had no real effect on Celia. "It's been hours. What's taking so long?"

Angel squealed and tried to shield Celia behind her body. "You're not supposed to see the bride before the ceremony!"

"The damn ceremony is beginning and everyone is in here."

Dane laughed out loud, shaking his head and taking his wife's hand. "Leave him be, honey. He's got it bad." He tugged Angel away, then out the door. To Alec he muttered, "You really ought to get a grip."

Alec stepped forward and lifted Celia into his arms. "Now that I have a grip on you, maybe we can get this show on the road." Without hesitation, he started out the door.

Celia tucked her face into his throat. "It's pretty unorthodox for the bride to be carried to the altar by the groom. What will people think?"

"That I love you and don't want to wait anymore."

He made that statement in his usual certain, determined way, then followed Dane and Angel into the crowded hall.

Celia kissed his throat. "I suppose it's a little unorthodox also, for the bride to find out on the day of her wedding that she's going to be a mama, but then, we've never done things by the book."

Alec froze. Celia could feel him tremble before she got such a tight squeeze she had to squeak in protest. As Alec entered the main room, carrying Celia with no effort at all while kissing the breath right out of her, applause broke out. The organ music continued, and the baffled bridesmaids fell into step behind the groom.

Dane, laughing again, said, "What the hell," and went over to grab his wife, pulling her out of line and keeping her at his side. The rest of the procession, confused, merely found a spot to stand around Celia and Alec.

Celia's mother was thoroughly scandalized, but she couldn't quite keep the grin off her face. Little Grayson, Dane and Angel's son, cheered loudly next to his grandmother.

When the preacher cleared his throat—twice— Alec finally managed to release Celia from the kiss. But against her mouth he whispered, "You just can't help but constantly take me off guard, can you?"

And Celia, laughing and crying and ruining her carefully applied makeup, kissed him again and said, "It's what I do best, Alec."

He stared at her mouth, ignored the snickering in the audience, the coughing of the preacher, and Dane's outright laughter. He answered, "Oh, I wouldn't exactly say that...."

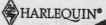

HARLEQUIN®

Temptation

There are *Babies*...
Cute! *Lovable!* *A handful!*

Then there are **BACHELORS**...
CUTE! SEXY! DEFINITELY A HANDFUL!

What happens when our heroines suddenly
have to deal with *both*?
Find out in the fun new miniseries

BACHELORS & BABIES...

#741 **The Badge and the Baby** Alison Kent (Aug. '99)
#745 **Baby.com** Molly Liholm (Sept. '99)
#749 **The Littlest Stowaway** Gina Wilkins (Oct. '99)
#753 **Oh, Baby!** Leandra Logan (Nov. '99)
#757 **The Good, the Bad and the Cuddly**
Heather MacAllister (Dec. '99)
and more to come!

Available at your favorite retail outlet.

HARLEQUIN®
Makes any time special ™

Look us up on-line at: http://www.romance.net   HTEB&B2

If you enjoyed what you just read,
then we've got an offer you can't resist!

Take 2 bestselling love stories FREE!

Plus get a FREE surprise gift!

Clip this page and mail it to Harlequin Reader Service®

IN U.S.A.	IN CANADA
3010 Walden Ave.	P.O. Box 609
P.O. Box 1867	Fort Erie, Ontario
Buffalo, N.Y. 14240-1867	L2A 5X3

YES! Please send me 2 free Harlequin Temptation® novels and my free surprise gift. Then send me 4 brand-new novels every month, which I will receive months before they're available in stores. In the U.S.A., bill me at the bargain price of $3.12 plus 25¢ delivery per book and applicable sales tax, if any*. In Canada, bill me at the bargain price of $3.57 plus 25¢ delivery per book and applicable taxes**. That's the complete price and a savings of over 10% off the cover prices—what a great deal! I understand that accepting the 2 free books and gift places me under no obligation ever to buy any books. I can always return a shipment and cancel at any time. Even if I never buy another book from Harlequin, the 2 free books and gift are mine to keep forever. So why not take us up on our invitation. You'll be glad you did!

142 HEN CNEV
342 HEN CNEW

Name	(PLEASE PRINT)	
Address	Apt.#	
City	State/Prov.	Zip/Postal Code

* Terms and prices subject to change without notice. Sales tax applicable in N.Y.
** Canadian residents will be charged applicable provincial taxes and GST.
   All orders subject to approval. Offer limited to one per household.
   ® are registered trademarks of Harlequin Enterprises Limited.

TEMP99   ©1998 Harlequin Enterprises Limited

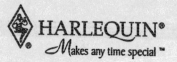 **HARLEQUIN®**
Makes any time special ™

 WIN A DREAM

In celebration of Harlequin®'s golden anniversary

Enter to win a *dream!* You could win:

- A luxurious trip for two to *The Renaissance Cottonwoods Resort* in Scottsdale, Arizona, or
- A bouquet of flowers once a week for a year from FTD, or
- A $500 shopping spree, or
- A fabulous bath & body gift basket, including K-tel's *Candlelight and Romance* 5-CD set.

Look for **WIN A DREAM** flash on specially marked Harlequin® titles by Penny Jordan, Dallas Schulze, Anne Stuart and Kristine Rolofson in October 1999*.

FTD

RENAISSANCE.
COTTONWOODS RESORT
SCOTTSDALE, ARIZONA

K·TEL

*No purchase necessary—for contest details send a self-addressed envelope to Harlequin Makes Any Time Special Contest, P.O. Box 9069, Buffalo, NY, 14269-9069 (include contest name on self-addressed envelope). Contest ends December 31, 1999. Open to U.S. and Canadian residents who are 18 or over. Void where prohibited.

PHMATS-GR

"This book is DYNAMITE!"
—Kristine Rolofson

"A riveting page turner..."
—Joan Elliott Pickart

"Enough twists and turns to keep everyone guessing... What a ride!"
—Jule McBride

See what all your favorite authors are talking about.

Coming October 1999 to a retail store near you.

HARLEQUIN®
Makes any time special ™

Silhouette®

In October 1999

MARIE FERRARELLA IS *Crazy for You*

Sparks fly and emotions soar as three unlikely couples pursue their mysterious attractions.

Bestselling author **Marie Ferrarella** proves opposites attract in three enticing stories about unexpected love.

Look for Marie Ferrarella's
Crazy For You in October 1999.

Available at your favorite retail outlet.

Silhouette ®

Visit us at www.romance.net

PSBR31099

No one can anticipate the unexpected,
be it lust, love or larceny...

SOMETHING TO HIDE

Two exciting
full-length novels by

TESS
GERRITSEN

and

LYNN
ERICKSON

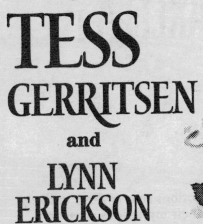

Intrigue and romance are combined in
this thrilling collection of heart-stopping
adventure with a guaranteed happy ending.

Available October 1999 at your favorite retail outlet.

HARLEQUIN®
Makes any time special™

Visit us at www.romance.net

PSBR21099

Every Man Has His Price!
HEART OF THE WEST

At the heart of the West there are a dozen rugged bachelors—up for auction!

This November 1999, look for
It Takes a Cowboy
by Gina Wilkins

Blair Townsend never knew how much she appreciated her organized life until her brother dumped his terror of a son on her doorstep. Blair decides he needs a positive role model—and the bachelor auction is the perfect place to find one. Scott McVey is perfect! Little does Blair know that her sophisticated businessman is really a wild and crazy rancher! Blair is forced to decide if Scott is good for her nephew…or for her.

Each book features a sexy new bachelor up for grabs—and a woman determined to rope him in!

Available at your favorite retail outlet.

HARLEQUIN®
Makes any time special™

Visit us at www.romance.net

PHHOW5

Temptation®

COMING NEXT MONTH

#753 OH, BABY! Leandra Logan
Bachelors & Babies

Die-hard bachelor Dylan Johnson had never forgotten—or forgiven—beautiful Allison Walker for walking out on him. But when the resourceful nanny showed up with a cuddly baby in tow, needing help, his heart thawed. And when he learned how much trouble she was in, Dylan was ready to give up his own bed...though he was sorely tempted to join her there!

#754 THE DADDY DECISION Donna Sterling
15ᵗʰ Anniversary Celebration!

Laura Merritt wanted a baby—no strings attached. Her friend Fletcher would make the perfect donor...er...daddy. Announcing her plans at their college reunion *seemed* like a good idea. But she hadn't counted on running into former flame Cort Dimitri who was determined that *he* should father her child—the old-fashioned way.

#755 HER SECRET LOVER Judith Arnold

Martha Cooper was in love with the boss, but Blake Robey was out of her league. She was shy and plain—he was one hundred percent male animal. Then one night she dreamed he made love to her—passionate, incredible love—but it wasn't real. So why was Blake looking at her as if he *were* her secret lover...?

#756 HOT AND BOTHERED Jo Leigh
Blaze

Only *one* woman in Manhattan got Trevor Templeton hot and bothered—gorgeous, leggy Lee Phillips. Unfortunately she was also Trevor's best friend, confidante and Sunday brunch partner. Making love with her could change all that...bring on all kinds of expectations. But wouldn't *one* night be worth it?

CNM1099